THE
DEPARTED

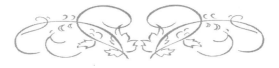

A MacKinnon Curse Novel

The Departed, A MacKinnon Curse novel, book three by J.A. Templeton

Copyright 2013 @ Julia Templeton

ISBN: 978-1480180512

1. Psychic ability-Fiction 2. Ghosts-Fiction 3. Horror-Fiction 4. Love-Fiction 5. Supernatural-Fiction 6. Self-Mutilation-Fiction

Cover Illustration by Kimberly Killion

Cover Photograph by Korie Nicole Photography (male cover model: Blake Williams)

Cover Photograph by Amanda Johansen (female cover model: Amanda Johansen)

Editing by Bulletproofing

Formatting by Tracy Cooper-Posey

THE
DEPARTED

A MacKinnon Curse Novel

Book 3

J.A. Templeton

To my wonderful readers—
Thank you for your support...and for loving my characters
as much as I do.
I appreciate you SO much!

Chapter One

The lights in my room were off, and the few candles gave off an eerie glow. For whatever reason, my friends thought it would be a good idea to bring a Ouija board to the slumber party.

As Cait set up the board, warning bells went off in my head, but apparently I was the only one who was concerned. Both Cass and Megan were eating popcorn and laughing, while taking sips off a fifth of rum that Cass had stolen from her stepmother.

Cait, wearing a wife-beater and pajama pants with skulls and crossbones, sat on her knees in front of the board. Hands resting on knees, she was all business. "Lightly touch your fingertips to this white plastic thing here."

"It's called a planchette," Cass blurted.

Cait rolled her eyes. "Place your fingers on the *planchette*. We'll ask spirits to contact us and they will communicate through the board."

This was all kinds of wrong; I felt it deep in my bones. Megan glanced at me. Was it my imagination, or was she a little hesitant? Cass obediently placed her fingers on the planchette.

I followed their lead.

We were quite the eclectic group with our pajama selection. Megan wore slightly thready flannel pajamas, Cass wore a silk and lace number that looked like something her stepmum would have worn, while I'd thrown on a white long-sleeved shirt and an old pair of faded sweats.

"We invite any spirits to join us tonight," Cait said in such a serious tone, Cass and Megan immediately cracked up.

Cait scowled at them. "Be serious, you two."

Unable to shake my misgivings, I took my fingers off the planchette. "I don't know about this. I just don't think—"

"You can watch if you're uncomfortable," Cait said, her tone made it seem like she was almost daring me to participate.

I *so* wasn't comfortable. "Are you sure you don't mind if I sit this one out?"

Cass did her typical eye roll. "Buzzkill," she muttered playfully under her breath.

Damn, I was tired of being considered a buzzkill because I didn't drink or want to play with a Ouija board.

Megan flashed a sympathetic smile my way.

I put my hands in my lap and inched back away from the board.

The seconds ticked away into a minute, and then another. The only thing that I could hear was the sound of my heart pounding in my ears.

Cait shifted a little. "Anyone who wants to communicate with us, please do so now. Use the planchette that we're all touching—to speak. Let us know that you can hear us."

It was obvious this wasn't Cait's first time with a Ouija board. She was totally into it, even focusing on her breathing, inhaling deeply, and then releasing in a steady rhythm. I was surprised, especially given the fact how sheltered her home life seemed to be. I couldn't imagine Mrs. MacKinnon allowing her kids to summon spirits.

Again, nothing happened. We all just sat bug-eyed staring at the board. Then, ever so slowly, the air around us turned freezing cold.

Megan's eyes widened in alarm and she brushed her hands up and down her arms. "Do you feel that?"

"What?" Cass asked, frowning. Apparently she didn't feel anything.

"Are you female?" Cait asked, excitement in her voice.

The planchette moved toward *NO*.

I breathed a sigh of relief.

"What is your name?" Cass said slowly. "Please spell it out letter by letter."

P-E-T-E-R.

Cait stole a glance at me, reminding me I had told her about Peter that day at the football game when she'd asked me if I could see spirits.

I sat up straighter and instantly relaxed. If Peter was here, then why didn't he show himself to me? Aside from the school, he seemed to steer clear of homes and other buildings. Even when he'd walked with me to the castle one day, he had stayed at the property line.

Realizing he might just be a little gun-shy, I took heart that we were dealing with a benevolent spirit and started to relax. Who knew, maybe this wouldn't be so bad after all...

Abruptly, the planchette moved to the side of the board, and the arrow pointed directly at me.

"I think he wants to communicate with you, Riley," Megan said, brown eyes wide.

I wondered if I should tell Cass and Megan that I knew of a boy spirit named Peter...or maybe I needed to just keep quiet for now.

Since Cait didn't bring the subject up, I decided to not say anything.

Megan cleared her throat. "Peter, how old are you?"

The planchette moved to the number one and then one again.

"Eleven," the three said in unison, and I smiled inwardly.

Yep, we had my Peter all right.

The planchette moved again. "R-I-L-E-Y," everyone said together.

Megan smiled. "Um, I think he likes you, Ri."

I grinned. I liked him, too.

"How did you die, Peter?" Cass asked, her excitement obvious to everyone.

M-U-R-D-E-R-E-D.

I frowned. Okay, the spirit must not be my Peter. He wouldn't have told me he'd died from tuberculosis if he'd been murdered, right? Unless I'd heard him wrong. Had I gotten the information messed up with someone else he'd been talking about, like a family member? I thought back over our conversation and I could swear he'd said he'd died of the illness.

And what were the chances of there being two ghosts by the name of Peter that were eleven years old?

Cait cleared her throat. "Peter, how were you murdered?"

The planchette didn't budge.

I glanced up at Cait, whose brows furrowed together. "Maybe he's afraid to tell us."

A putrid odor filled my nostrils, making bile rise in my throat. I looked around at my friends, wondering why they weren't reacting to it. Unless...I was the only one who could smell it.

"Who murdered you?" Cait asked. Our gazes met for a second. Had I told her how Peter had died?

The planchette moved at lightning speed.

M-A-C-K-I-N-N-O-N.

M-A-C-K-I-N-N-O-N.

M-A-C-K-I-N-N-O-N.

Cait jerked her hands away from the planchette. She glanced at me. "Tell me this isn't some kind of sick joke."

I shook my head. "I swear."

She turned to Cass and Megan. Their eyes were huge and they shook their heads adamantly, their hands now in their laps. "We swear."

"You're the one who brought the Ouija board here, Cait," Cass said, stating the obvious, and looking pissed off that Cait would even accuse her of such a thing.

Cait's throat contracted as she swallowed hard.

Obviously Peter hadn't been killed by the MacKinnons, but I knew who had been...apparently the same ghost who was pretending to be a sweet, eleven-year-old boy that I had befriended. I thought back on all the things I had said to Peter, how I'd confided in him and how I'd truly believed he was a young boy who had died of an illness before he'd had a chance to grow to adulthood.

What a heinous thing for Laria to do, but what did I expect? We were talking about the same ghost who had masqueraded as my dead mother, possessed my brother and my friend, and made Kade believe he was with me the night of Tom's party instead of with Dana.

Laria was ruthless. In fact, what else had she done that I wasn't even aware of?

"Is there a MacKinnon here now?" Cass asked.

Cait's mouth was wide open. "What are you doing?"

The planchette moved by itself, toward Cait, then slowly spelled out M-A-C-K-I-N-N-O-N.

"Oh shit," Cass said under her breath.

"What year did you die?" I asked, my heart pounding hard, but needing to know the answer.

The planchette moved slowly toward the numbers. Stopping at the number one, then at the seven, then eight, then six.

I felt the blood drain from my face.

"1786." Cait sat back, and I could see her grappling for an answer. "That's over two hundred years ago."

"Your name isn't Peter, is it?" I asked before I could stop myself. I needed to know the truth.

All three of my friends' heads whipped toward me, and I clearly saw the confusion on their faces.

NO.

It felt like someone had hit me in the gut. "Your name is Laria, isn't it?"

"Who the fuck is Laria?" Cass asked, her voice mirroring the fear on her face.

I wasn't surprised, especially since a similar fear consumed me.

"She was a servant who practiced witchcraft and died at the castle a couple hundred years ago," Cait said solemnly. "She poisoned an ancestor of mine, Ian MacKinnon, and his family hung her and buried her on unhallowed ground."

"Bloody hell," Cass said, looking horrified. "A witch? But that still doesn't explain how Riley knew, though."

"Meg and Cass, do you remember the woman we saw on our way home from Aberdeen?"

Cass and Megan glanced at each other and nodded.

"That woman was Laria, a spirit who has been haunting me since I moved here."

Cass came slowly to her feet. "This is too twisted for me. I mean, if you came up with this to scare me, props to you, because it worked."

"I'm not making it up," I said, sounding as tired as I felt. "I wish I was."

Megan reached for Cass's hand and pulled her back down beside her.

"You're fucking serious, aren't you?" Cass asked.

Without a word, Megan reached for the fifth and took a long drink. She wiped her mouth with the back of her hand, her gaze settling on me. "I didn't say anything to either of you. I was too afraid to, but she touched me that day...and her hands were like ice. Her face was so pale. Like an unearthly white. I felt so many weird thoughts and feelings race through me in that moment."

I remembered Megan acting a bit off after that encounter. Had Laria been possessing her from that point? I wondered. I wished I could bring up the ride home from the game tonight, the way Laria had taken over Megan and drove the car without even looking at the road...and the creepy way her head had twisted around toward the headrest. But I knew it would be too much for any of my friends to hear right now, especially Megan, so I kept the information to myself.

"What does Peter have to do with Laria? I don't get it," Megan said, stealing a concerned glance at Cass, who looked ready to bolt for the door.

"I think that Peter is actually Laria," I blurted.

"Wait?" Cait said, scrambling to her feet. "What?"

Cass took a swig and handed the bottle to Cait, who didn't mess around and took three large gulps before handing it to Megan.

Megan took a swallow and handed it to me. I took a sip, and winced as the liquor burned its way down my throat. I handed the fifth to Cass.

"What do we do now?" Megan asked.

"What do you want, Laria?" I asked, and held my breath expectantly, waiting for the response.

D-E-A-T-H.

My heart dropped to my toes.

"Whose death?" Cass asked, before anyone could stop her.

A-L-L-O-F-Y-O-U.

Chapter Two

"Oh, hell no," Cass said, taking the planchette and throwing it across the room where it hit the wall with a thud. "No fucking way."

She was looking at me, wanting answers where, unfortunately, I didn't have any.

Cait, who was the calmest of everyone, slid her hands down her face. "I'm sorry. I shouldn't have brought the board. What a mistake."

"Ya think?" Cass said, shaking her head. "Tell me this is bullshit because I am ready to walk out the door."

"It's not a joke, Cass. I wish it were." I stood and walked over to the bed, moved the pillow out of the way where they could see the word 'DIE' carved into my headboard.

"This *ghost* did that?" Megan asked, her voice skeptical.

I nodded. "Yeah, she did."

"Why didn't you tell us?" Cass asked.

"Because you wouldn't understand," Cait replied, crossing her arms over her chest. "Would you tell anyone, especially people you've just met?"

"Probably not," Cass muttered.

I was so relieved that at least Cait understood. I didn't feel quite so alone.

Megan had become pretty quiet, though.

I was desperate to tell them everything—that Laria had possessed Shane and Megan, and that she was possibly behind the death of Anne Marie, my housekeeper's best friend, who had summoned Laria when she had first started haunting me. But now that Laria had left her not-so-subtle threat to kill all of us, I needed to weigh my options to avoid their freaking out on me.

"How do we know you didn't carve 'DIE' into the headboard?" Megan asked, her voice calm, her stare cold.

"That's such a fucked up thing to say," Cass said, frowning at Megan. "You always give me shit about saying the wrong thing, but seriously—that was low."

Megan stared blankly at her. "What? I mean...she cuts."

Cait gasped. "Jesus, Meg."

Megan would never say something so mean. I knew that. There was just no way. Heat raced to my cheeks because all three girls were staring at me, waiting for my response. It was all out on the table now. I had nothing else to hide.

"You're right, Megan, I do cut...but I'm trying to quit." I cleared my throat. Despite the fact Megan was acting sketchy, these were my friends, my best friends, and I needed to be completely honest with them. "I started cutting over a year ago after my mom died. I didn't know how to deal with my pain, and for whatever reason—even if it doesn't make sense to you—it was one way for me to release my pain. I hate that I've done it. I hate that it eats at me."

Not one of them looked surprised by my admission, making me

wonder who else, aside from Dana and her crew, had made it a point to harass me about cutting.

"You don't owe us an explanation," Cait said, as she reached for my hand and squeezed it. "None of us can relate to what you've been through in your life. I can't imagine losing my mum. Just know that we're your friends and we'll help you whenever you need us."

The sides of Megan's mouth lifted the slightest bit, and though she had brown eyes, they were darker than I recalled. I wasn't about to call Laria out in front of Cass and Cait. I didn't want them freaking out even more than they already were.

"I'm glad you were honest with us. That says a lot," Cass said. The words filled me with relief.

"Me, too," Cait said, glancing at Megan.

Megan picked a piece of lint off the rug, staring at me in that messed-up way. I felt like at any second she would leap across the room and jump me.

"Thanks, guys." I cleared my throat, needing to lay it all on the line. "I want to also warn you about something—that spirits can masquerade inside people who are living."

Cass set down on my bed. "Masquerade in the living? Like how?"

"Like possession?" Cait asked.

"Yes, like possession," I said. "The person may not even know they are being taken over. There could be times where they just don't feel like themselves, like being pissed off or PMSing for no reason. There could even be episodes where they black out and don't remember anything...and we're talking for a period of time."

Cass's eyes narrowed. "Like how long a period of time?"

"I don't know for sure," I replied, choosing my words carefully. "But it takes energy for a spirit to manifest and gain enough power to manipulate the living."

Cait gave a shudder. "Creepy."

"How do you know so much about possession?" Cass lifted her feet off the floor, as though she was terrified someone would reach out from under the bed and grab her.

"Cait already knows this." I turned to Cass and Megan. "I'm being haunted by Laria, but I see more spirits than just her. In fact, I've been able to see the dead since the accident that killed my mom."

Cass glanced at me. "So...what's it like?"

I shrugged. "It's kind of like seeing you guys...sometimes ghosts are transparent, and sometimes they are as solid as any human being. Some ghosts are nice and just want to be noticed, while there are others—dark spirits—who can make life miserable."

"Like Laria?" Cait said.

I nodded. "Like Laria."

Three quick knocks sounded at my door and we all jumped.

I prayed my dad hadn't been standing outside the door. I put a finger to my lips, walked to the door and, with a steadying breath, opened it.

Shane held a plate of cookies. "Compliments of Miss A," he said, and the entire mood of the room shifted. Megan still sat sullen, but Cass was up off the bed and walked toward Shane, playing with a strand of hair while swishing her hips.

His gaze slowly slid over her, taking in the silk pajamas and lifting an appreciative brow.

Cait stiffened, apparently jealous of the attention Shane was giving Cass. I knew Cait really liked Shane. Everyone knew it, but to her credit, she wasn't too obvious.

Shane's gaze shifted to Cait a second later. The corners of his mouth curved as he checked out the skull pajama pants and tight camisole, and then their gazes met.

Yep, there were some smoldering stares going on between the two.

I looked at Megan, and if I'd wondered whether Laria was in the room before, I had no question of it now. She didn't seem at all bothered by the interaction between Cait and Shane, and normally the jealousy would have been written all over her face.

"Thanks," I said, taking the plate from him.

Cait shifted on her feet. "You want to hang out with us?"

Shane brushed a hand through his already disheveled blond hair. He glanced at me and I shrugged. Honestly, I didn't care. In fact, given the dark conversation we'd been having, I was only too happy to have him stay.

"Actually, I'm going to get cleaned up first, but maybe I'll hang with you later."

"We're going to watch a movie. Maybe you can watch it with us?" Cass said, her mood becoming more upbeat by the second.

All it took was Shane flashing a smile to ease everyone's fears. "How can I say no to a room full of beautiful women? Count me in."

I laughed under my breath, while Cass and Cait beamed.

"What's wrong, Meg?" Shane asked, and she glanced up, brows lifted high.

Megan shook her head. "Nothing."

His gaze abruptly shifted to the Ouija board. He looked at me and frowned.

"A stupid game," Cass said, kicking the board under the bed.

"Get rid of it," Shane said, his good mood gone.

"I will," I promised, as I reached for it.

An arm abruptly grabbed me and yanked me under the bed.

My friends' screams filled the room.

Strong hands, which had to belong to Shane, gripped my ankles and pulled, but the person who had my arms yanked right back with even more force. My shoulders felt like they were being ripped from the sockets.

I was scared to open my eyes, because if Laria was possessing Megan, then who exactly was holding on to me?

More hands joined my brother's, and as I felt my friends and Shane gain the upper hand, I found the courage to peek at my assailant.

It was Laria and her eyes were full of rage. "Pain and death," she said, in that unearthly tone I heard in my nightmares. Her nails dug into the skin at my arms, clawing harder as Shane and the girls tugged hard, freeing me from Laria's grasp.

Before I could blink, Shane's hands were on my shoulders. "Are you okay?"

My heart was pounding so loud I barely heard him. I nodded.

Cass's mouth was wide open. Cait looked ready to throw up, and Megan still sat in the same spot. She hadn't bothered to help at all.

"Who are you?" I asked Megan, and everyone looked at her, confusion on their faces.

"What do you mean?" Megan asked, as she slowly came to her feet. "I'm your friend."

"Riley?—" Shane started.

I shook my head. "There's a spirit inside Megan, and I'm guessing it wasn't Laria since she was the one who pulled me underneath the bed."

"Oh, hell no," Cass said, taking a step toward the door. "You're trying to tell me she's possessed?"

I nodded. Cait stayed rooted to the spot.

Shane stepped between me and Megan. "Who are you?"

A slow, menacing smile crossed Megan's lips. "I am your worst nightmare." The voice wasn't Megan's. It was deep and masculine... like Randall's voice, the creepy guy who had introduced Laria to the dark arts.

Cass screamed and Cait took Shane's hand.

"You have no power here," I said with a force that surprised me. "This is my home and you are not welcome here. Leave now."

"Leave now!" Cait said with me, and soon everyone in the room was repeating the words over and over again.

The spirit in Megan began to laugh, a deep-throated horrific chuckle that sent shivers along my spine. I was proud of Cait, Cass, and Shane. They kept repeating the words along with me, and soon Megan was backing up against the wall.

Her gaze abruptly shifted to the right, where beside the window I saw a bright figure. I couldn't make out who it was, but I felt the energy move through me like a wave. A positive wave that grew stronger by the second.

I received an image of Anne Marie in my vision, along with one of my mom. She was still with me. What a relief it was to see and feel her, and know she had my back.

"What's going on?" Megan looked at us, her brow furrowed as her gaze shifted over each of us. "You're freaking me out. Say something."

She was acting like Megan, and I noticed her eyes didn't look so dark.

Cass went to her bag, took three gulps off the fifth. "Oh my God, I'm never going to sleep again."

"It's okay," I said as I gave Megan a hug, relieved to have my friend back.

She hugged me, and then looked at my arms. "What happened?"

There were long scratch marks down the length of both arms, and a couple of them were bleeding.

"That Laria bitch yanked her under the bed, and when she came out, she had those scratches," Cass said, glancing at Shane. "Do you have a joint? I need to get blazed."

"You think getting high is a good idea, and who the hell is Laria?" Megan asked.

Yep, our Megan was back.

"Um, it's definitely a good idea," Cait replied. "I'm right there with you."

"Crack the window," I said, then thought better of it. I didn't know what Laria would do, especially after the threat that each of us would die. An open window was just giving her an invitation.

That, or I could imagine her hanging upside down in my window, like she had done to me weeks before. My friends would lose their minds.

Shane crossed the room, cracked the window slightly, and removed the wallet from his back pocket. He pulled out a joint and lit it. He inhaled deeply, held the hit in for a good fifteen seconds, before he exhaled the smoke out into the pitch-black night.

Cass approached him, and took the joint right out of his fingers. He sat down in the chair and glanced at me. We were in deep shit and he knew it. I was grateful he was here, helping calm down my friends, but then what? How were we going to move forward? What could we do to get rid of Laria, Randall, and the others?

Cait must have E.S.P., because she said, "Couldn't we do like an exorcism or something?"

Anne Marie would have been helpful when it came to exorcising negative spirits. Now I was clueless as to who to ask, and I didn't feel comfortable walking into a church and asking the clergy for help.

The last thing I needed was a priest talking to my dad right now.

I was on shaky ground with Dad as it was. Talk of ghosts, even with Shane backing me up, would have me thrown into a mental ward.

"Shane, will you do us a favor and look under the bed?" Cait asked after they'd finished smoking. Even Megan had given in and taken one hit.

None of them looked any more relaxed. In fact, I think the weed might have had a less than calming effect on Cass, who was chewing her fingernails off.

"Sure," Shane said, going down on his knees. He reached underneath the bed, and pulled out the Ouija board. "First things first, though. We're getting rid of this."

Chapter Three

My friends finished off the entire plate of cookies, then rummaged through the kitchen cabinets and refrigerator looking for munchies. The best way to counteract the nightmare of Laria yanking me beneath the bed and possessing Megan was a solid dose of comic relief, compliments of Scottish cable. We sat huddled on the couch together, with Shane sprawled in the chair beside us.

Dad came in about eleven thirty. Everyone had put eye drops in their bloodshot eyes, but they remained quiet while Dad asked a few questions. Thankfully, he gave up and headed to his room.

At three in the morning, I was having a tough time keeping my eyes open. Plus, I'd had all the comedy I could handle and excused myself, saying I needed to sleep. Megan followed me, and Cass and Cait said they'd be right behind us.

I brushed my teeth, and fell into bed beside an already snoring Megan. I kept the bathroom light on and left the door open...just in case. I lay awake for thirty minutes, staring at the ceiling, exhausted mind racing. I heard Cass tell Shane and Cait goodnight. I closed my eyes as she snuggled beside me. Sandwiched between my friends, I slowly drifted off to sleep.

I could barely make out the fire from where I stood in the forest, hidden behind a thick outcropping of trees. The place was unfamiliar to me: dense, cold, and dark.

Roughly thirty feet away a group of at least twenty people, all wearing long black robes, stood before a raging fire. In the center I could see an altar, a velvet drape slung over the rock slab, and a goblet in the center.

The hair on the back of my neck stood on end, and I glanced over my shoulder to make sure I hadn't been followed. I was scared to death at what I was witnessing firsthand.

A low chanting began with the males in the group, and soon the women joined in. I was in way over my head. I felt it, and yet I knew if I moved I risked the chance of someone discovering me. I crouched down lower, crawled slowly behind a fallen tree, and settled in amongst the ferns on the forest floor.

The chanting ended abruptly, and for a second I thought maybe I'd been discovered. I heard the rustle of brush off to my right. Two men approached and between them there was a slim, blindfolded woman with long, golden blonde hair.

The closer they came to the crowd, the more panicked the woman became, fighting against her captors. Her efforts were useless. The two men laughed and tightened their hold.

I barely breathed, too afraid they would see me as they came closer to my hiding spot, not even five feet away from where they passed by.

I tucked my hair inside my hood. That slight movement made a twig beneath me crunch and the men stopped. The blood roared in my ears. I closed my eyes, praying they would continue walking by.

"Come quickly," a sharp voice said from the circle of onlookers. Eve-

ryone looked in my direction. The men pulled the woman along down the pathway, toward the certain doom that awaited her. I felt her anxiety, her confusion, and I wanted to step out, to save her…but I was helpless. Instead, I cowered in my hiding spot, watching.

A tall man stepped forward out of the group and the crowd made a circle around him. "Welcome, friends."

For the next twenty minutes I didn't move an inch while I listened to a sick ritual, spoken in a language I didn't recognize. The group recited certain words the leader said. The blindfolded woman was pushed to her knees, her arms tied securely behind her.

The blindfold was removed and the woman's wild gaze took everything in with a glance. Even from where I was, I could see the fear and terror in her eyes as she realized she was surrounded.

The tall man motioned one of the captors forward. The man produced a knife from within his robes. The girl put her hands up at the same time the man thrust. His blade made contact with her wrist, cutting deeply.

She cried out in pain. The crowd began to chant once again, this time in a more frenzied way. The girl was lifted up onto the altar, and I could see her trembling, no doubt in shock.

The tall man stepped forward and, taking the blade from the other man, sliced the victim's other wrist in a slashing, brutal fashion. With a triumphant smile, he lifted her arm up and with great ceremony let the blood gush into the goblet. He brought the goblet to his lips and drank deeply, while the onlookers stood in god-like worship.

When he was finished, he handed the goblet to the person to his right. On and on the ritual went, until every last person drank. The leader motioned for someone to step forward from the crowd. I made out Laria, and the man at the center, the leader, was Randall Cummins. I felt like someone had hit me square in the gut. The leader of the coven *was a servant in the MacKinnon household.*

Laria seemed hesitant to drink, but with Randall's nod, she did. When they were finished, his hand found hers, holding her tight.

I saw something pass between them. She looked at him with adulation, as did many of the followers. Randall was at least a decade older than she was, but what passed between them was a smoldering expression that couldn't be misinterpreted.

Unable to stand the sight, my gaze shifted to the victim on the altar who seemed to have accepted her fate. She didn't move at all. In fact, I wondered if she was already dead. Just then she shifted slightly. What must be going through her mind as her life slipped away? I wondered. From a distance she looked no older than me. No older than Laria. Her honey-colored hair was in disarray around her shoulders, arms flung out to her sides, blood dripping onto the ground.

Another thirty minutes ticked by, and finally, with the dying light of the fire and a few carefully chosen words by Randall, the group started to disperse and headed out of the woods. The two men who had dragged the victim here wrapped the girl up in the drape, and the stockier man flung her over his shoulder.

I stayed in my crouched position, too afraid to do anything except breathe short, shallow breaths. There were too many of them, and I couldn't afford to be sighted, so I lowered my head, hoping I had managed to disappear completely into the landscape. The steps of the group grew heavier, close to me, and I was scared that someone would be able to hear my racing heart or discover me.

I didn't move for a while after hearing the last person pass by. When I lifted my head, I sighed with relief. Everyone was gone, and the fire was extinguished. All that was left was the scent of smoke from the fire, and the stone where the makeshift altar had been placed.

"Who are you?"

I jumped, horrified I'd been discovered.

I lifted my head, and staring back at me was the girl who had been on the altar. I glanced at her wrists. There were no wounds.

I frowned. "I saw you being cut."

"They killed me," she said matter-of-factly. "I'm dead..."

You didn't stop them. *She didn't say it, but I felt the accusation anyway. Felt guilt consume me.*

"I'm so sorry," I whispered, terrified that someone would hear us, despite the fact that the forest had grown quiet.

"I have something to show you," she said, pointing toward the clearing, toward the moon just beyond in the sky. "Come." She tugged on my sleeve, pulled me further into the woods. We walked in the opposite direction of the others, and at a slight incline.

When she abruptly stopped and turned, we were at the very top of the hillside, looking down over the valley, toward the castle. From this vantage point you could see everything. The small clearing where the ritual had taken place, and then beyond toward the river and the castle, directly southwest.

We were far enough away from the castle that no one would hear the group as they chanted and sacrificed people.

"The witch is buried there," she said, pointing just over the hill, in the direction of thick brush overgrown with berry bushes, and the rugged stone that was the size of a basketball.

Someone had made sure to mark the grave.

"The witch? Who is the witch?"

"The one who haunts you."

I swallowed hard. But I had just seen Laria...and she'd been alive.

"How do you know it's her? She's alive. I just saw her."

"You're dreaming, Riley," she said with a soft smile. "Find her...and you find them all."

I glanced down at her hand, which gripped my wrist tighter. I tried to pull away, but as I watched, the skin pulled away from her hand, leaving nothing but bone. Her face hollowed out before my eyes, her flesh turned to dust.

I blinked and she was gone.

I woke in the early morning with Cass spooning me on one side, and Megan facing me, her arm around my waist. I lifted my head slightly, looking for Cait. My heart skittered when I didn't see her in the chair or on the floor.

It was safe to assume she was with Shane, especially since they'd been checking each other out all night. I needed to be sure, though...

I slid out from underneath Megan's arm. Cass moaned and rolled over, where Megan didn't move at all. I'd noticed last night after the Laria episode that Megan had been quiet, saying very little as she listened intently to Cass's play-by-play. I could tell she wanted to ask me questions, but I think a part of her was terrified to find out the truth. I couldn't blame her. Actually, I couldn't blame any of them if they wanted to run for the hills.

I went straight to Shane's room. I lifted my hand, ready to knock on the door, but I didn't want to wake up Miss A or, God forbid, Dad. Before I could talk myself out of it, I pushed the door open, took two steps in, and quickly shut it behind me.

Shane was shirtless, his arm wrapped around Cait who, from what I could tell, had her jammies on. Relieved that at least I'd located her, I took a step toward the door.

"What's up, Ri?" Shane asked, glancing at the clock on his nightstand with squinty eyes.

"Just looking for Cait."

He looked completely innocent, but I knew guys, and my little brother loved women. "She said your bed looked a little full."

True, my bed had been full with three of us squeezed onto a queen-size mattress. Given what had happened last night with Laria yanking me under the bed, I'm sure she wasn't up to sleeping on the floor. I wouldn't have been either, and what better excuse to cozy up with a guy you liked. If we'd been at Cait's house, I guarantee I would have found a way to spend the night with Kade.

"No need to explain," I said with a wink. "I'm heading back to bed, but tell Cait she might want to slip back into the room before Miss A or Dad wakes up. I don't want either one having a meltdown and putting an end to any future slumber parties."

"Got it," he said.

Cait kept her eyes shut, but I had a feeling she heard every single word.

I went back to bed, but I couldn't sleep. I kept thinking back over the dream. A million different questions raced in my mind. The woman I had seen—the one who had been killed at the witches' hands—it's like I felt her lingering presence. Had the dream been real, or just a figment of my imagination...a fear from my subconscious mind?

It bothered me about Randall and Laria. I didn't get that look that had passed between them, especially since she'd been so crazy for Ian she had killed him.

Frustrated, I took a shower and just stood for a few minutes with my eyes closed. When I heard movement in my room, I shampooed my hair and washed it out. I reached for the conditioner. My breath caught in my throat. My wrists were slashed and blood drained from the wounds onto the shower floor and swirled down the drain.

In the reflection of the faucet, I saw a figure standing behind me.

I swallowed a scream. Even though it was difficult to make out features in the distorted chrome, she resembled the blonde girl from the dream. The sacrificial lamb.

Her hand rested on my shoulder, and she squeezed lightly. "Find her and you find them all."

Those were the exact same words she'd said in my dream. She was gone a second later. I looked down at my wrists. No cuts and no blood anywhere. The water at my feet was completely clear.

Fear rippled along my spine.

Why had I seen the blood and slashed wrists? Was the spirit warning me that Laria was going to kill me, or rather, one day I might go too far if I continued cutting?

"Sorry, gotta pee," I heard Cass say, and I jumped. I hadn't even heard the bathroom door open.

"I must say, Ri…I slept pretty good last night."

"I'm glad," I said, conditioning my hair. I was in a hurry to get out of the shower before any other spirit made an appearance.

"Cait came tiptoeing in about five minutes ago," she said with a snort. "Busted." She flushed the toilet before I could tell her not to. Cold water caught me full in the face, and I stepped back out of the spray.

"I bet your brother's a great lay."

"Eww, keep your thoughts to yourself, please," I said, rinsing the conditioner from my hair and turning off the water.

"You and Cait banging each others' brothers. Keeping it all in the family."

"Stop it, already."

She laughed, obviously enjoying my discomfort. "Hey, leave the water running. I'm getting a shower in before Megan. That bitch can run a water heater bone dry, let me tell you."

I turned the faucet back on and grabbed my towel off the hook beside the shower. Cass was already naked. There were no modesty issues where she was concerned. She was brushing her hair and checking me out in the mirror. "Megan said you were meeting up with Kade today."

I slid my robe on and towel-dried my hair. "Yeah, I'll call him this afternoon."

"You two belong together. I mean, you're really good together, but I think you know that already."

I felt that we were good together and it was nice to hear that other people thought we were as well. "Thanks." I just didn't know how he was going to take the truth about my life, about all that happened, and if he would still feel the same about me after he heard everything.

"He's never been so into anyone. I mean, no one has had the effect you do on him. Honestly, it's kind of fascinating to watch."

I'd never been so into anyone either and I was excited to see Kade. I hated how things had been between us since the night of Tom's party, and in a strange way going through so much made me realize just how much I loved him. He would have never knowingly hurt me.

Megan walked in. She glanced at Cass and shook her head. "Um, okay you exhibitionist. Please get in the shower before I go blind from staring at your pasty white ass."

Cass flipped her off and made a production of ripping the shower curtain back.

"On that note, I'm gonna go get dressed," I said, stepping into my room and shutting the bathroom door behind me.

Cait, who had been looking out the window, turned and smiled. "Morning."

"How did you sleep?" I asked.

"Good, and you?"

"Well, considering I was wedged between Cass and Megan, I'd say fair."

The smile faded from her lips. "Ri, what are we going to do about Laria?"

Miss A pulled out all the stops with breakfast.

I sat at the table with my friends. We'd all taken showers and got cleaned up, but no one said much of anything now that we sat around the dining room table. Cass wolfed down her breakfast, Cait chewed on a piece of bacon, where Megan just managed to push her food around her plate as she kept glancing at Cait and Shane, who had joined us a few minutes ago.

Cait glanced toward the kitchen, where Miss A was cleaning up the dishes. "So, we need a plan of action."

She definitely didn't waste any time.

Cass set her fork down and wiped her mouth with the napkin. "I have to be honest here. I don't know how much help I can be. I mean, I'm completely in over my head in this. Granted, I know I told you once that I had seen my granddad's spirit and all, but this is some messed up shit." She lowered her voice. "I won't even watch any movies that deal with possession because they freak me out too much. And now there's a possibility that some insane ghost can mess with me and my friends. Um, no thanks."

I knew the feeling when it came to those movies. I'd always felt the same way. Now one of my greatest fears had become a reality. I wanted to tell them about the dream I'd had last night, about Laria's possible burial site, but I was still processing the dream and how to proceed.

The last thing I wanted was the five of us coming up with a half-assed plan to wander into the woods and go searching for a two-hundred-year-old grave. Even though we were in rural Scotland, the forests changed with time. Trees were larger, brush was denser. It would be like looking for a needle in a haystack.

While everyone was quiet and continued to eat, I did what I told myself I wouldn't do with my buddies. I decided to try and read their thoughts.

Megan was completely twisted. Her energy was scattered, and I could feel jealousy toward Cait coming off her in waves. I still didn't quite understand why she was so jealous when she was clearly in love with Milo. I'm sure what she felt for Shane was a crush, but I wished that crush would go away because it would only make things more awkward. Maybe if Cait and Shane ended up together, that would put a fork in it for her.

Reading Cass, I could tell there was a part of her that was actually kind of into the ghost hunting part of what we were going through, and yet she was terrified, which was understandable. Going from seeing a ghost to talking ghost possession was a lot to accept.

Cait was the toughest of my friends to read. She seemed overly calm. Too calm in some ways. Then again, she might just be processing everything, especially since her family was so intimately involved. Her mind kept skipping to Shane, and I had to smile to myself, knowing that she was really into him.

Shane took a drink of juice. "Everyone just needs to stay vigilant and if you see or experience anything, to let all of us know."

Everyone seemed in a better mood by the time they left my house just before noon. I went to the back patio and looked over at the hillside beyond the castle. Somewhere up in those woods was Laria's grave.

Find her, and you find them all.

That warning would stay in my head for as long as I lived.

Chapter Four

At ten minutes after one I finally texted Kade and told him I was ready to talk. Five minutes later the doorbell rang. Honestly, I was happy to know he was as anxious to talk to me as I was to talk to him.

I glanced at my reflection in the mirror. I had made an effort to look my best. My hair hadn't been cooperating, so I had slicked it back in a high ponytail, and wore a flowy cream shirt with a pair of cobalt blue slim-fitting pants and cute flats.

Kade knocked and I opened the door. His gaze skimmed my body and slowly lifted to meet mine. A boyish smile spread across his lips and my stomach did a flip.

His navy button-down shirt was rolled up at the elbows and open at the neck, exposing part of his strong chest and the Celtic cross necklace, like the one I wore. He had on my favorite jeans, too...the ones that cupped his butt in the nicest possible way.

I was toast.

All the reasons I had come up with to put our relationship on hold evaporated. I wanted to slide into his arms and tell him immediately that everything would be okay. That all was forgiven, and yet I stopped myself short of doing that.

I already knew the reason behind his infidelity, and though it was Laria's handiwork, the video of him hooking up with Dana had been permanently burned into my brain. There was a part of me that felt betrayed and I guess I wasn't ready to jump back in with both feet...even though my heart was telling me to do exactly that. The fact of the matter was, regardless of the circumstances, he'd been with someone else, and I hated it. Hated the thought that he had shared what we had shared with someone else...*after* we had been together. The girls who had come before me didn't matter, but Dana—oh my God, I hated her with a passion. And as much as I wanted to forget, my mind tried to fill in the blanks of what the video had missed...and that would happen every single time I saw Dana.

"Hey," he said, going back on his heels. "You had said to come by...hopefully I'm not appearing too eager."

"You didn't waste any time," I said with a soft laugh that seemed to ease the tension.

"Who's here?" my dad asked from his office.

"Kade," I said, hand on the door handle. "You want to go somewhere and talk?"

I didn't want to be in my house. I felt like the walls were closing in on me and I needed to put some distance between me and the inn.

Kade nodded. "Yeah."

I knew just the place. I shut the front door and started walking toward the hill where I had hung out with Ian, keeping a few feet of distance between us as we rounded the inn toward the back.

As we walked in silence, I felt Kade's gaze on me. A million different emotions raced through me, mostly concern that he wouldn't understand everything, but it was time to say what was on my mind.

The wind picked up the further we climbed, and I was glad I'd worn my hair in a pony. I focused on Kade and his thoughts. I could feel his nervousness, and the worry. He didn't know what to expect, and I didn't know where to start. I had told him yesterday that we had a lot to talk about...and we did. Plus, my friends knew everything now. Soon Kade would too. Would it change how he felt about me? Would he run for the hills once he learned the truth?

"How about here?" I asked when we were nearly at the top.

Kade raked a hand through his dark hair. "Sure," he said, following my lead as I sat down.

He picked a blade of grass, rolled it between finger and thumb. "Riley, I never meant to hurt you," he said, as he watched me closely. "I wish more than anything I could go back in time and erase that night."

I nodded. "I know."

"I hate myself for what happened. I thought it was you. I mean, it's so bizarre—because it's not like I was wasted or anything. But one second you were there, standing in front of me, and then when I woke up the next day I had this horrible feeling in the pit of my stomach."

"I know that, too."

His brows furrowed and he tossed the blade of grass aside. "I feel like you don't, though. You're saying you know it, but you act like you don't know. I feel the distance between us...and I hate it. I want back what we had."

If only that were possible.

My heart was hammering against my chest so hard it felt like it would burst. It was time to be completely honest. "This is really tough for me to say..."

I saw fear enter his eyes.

I cleared my throat. "You know how I asked you the other day about ghosts?"

I saw and felt his confusion. He nodded. "Yeah."

"Well, I can see ghosts...just like I see you. I sense them. I hear them. I talk to them."

It was obvious by his stunned expression he'd been expecting me to say something different. "You mean you're psychic?"

"Yes."

His eyes widened a little.

"And there's a spirit who is haunting me," I said, weighing my words carefully. "Someone who wants to hurt me."

He sat up straighter, his shoulders ramrod straight. "Hurt you... like how?"

I pressed my lips together and looked toward the inn, and then to the castle. "Like, kill me. Contrary to what some people believe, the dead can harm the living, but I should probably start at the beginning."

The nerve in his jaw ticked.

"Your ancestor, Ian MacKinnon, the one I talked about at your house the night I met your family—well, I met him when I first moved here."

His eyes narrowed as he watched me. "You met his ghost?"

I nodded.

"He's the one who is haunting you? The one who wants to hurt you?"

"No, God no. Sorry."

He visibly relaxed.

"Ian doesn't want to hurt me. It's that witch Laria who killed him. She is haunting me." I chewed on my fingernail. This was a train wreck. "I know this sounds crazy, but Laria wants revenge on me for helping Ian cross over to the light."

I knew it would be tough for anyone to understand, and Kade was doing his best to digest what I was saying, though I could see a kind of my-girlfriend-is-nuts expression flash across his face.

"You think I'm crazy," I said, before I could stop myself.

"No," he said, as he took my hand in his. "It's just a lot to take in."

Tears burned behind my eyes, and I guess I didn't realize just how exhausted I was until that moment. How tired I was of explaining myself to people I cared about, and having them look at me like I was crazy.

His thumb teased the hairs at the base of my neck. "Riley, I believe you."

Those words meant everything. What I wouldn't give to tell him that he was Ian in a past life, but it was hard to wrap your brain around the fact that you could be living at the same time your earthbound spirit was hanging out with your girlfriend. "There's more... Laria is able to manipulate people to do what she wants. Basically she can shift into people—and take them over."

"You mean possession?" Even his tone was full of disbelief.

"Yes."

His eyes went wide. "Are you saying the other night at the party..."

"That's exactly what I'm saying. She's done some really twisted things, trust me."

He cussed under his breath. "How is that possible?"

"It just is. Maybe there's witchcraft involved. I don't know. I mean, it's hard to believe."

"So that's why I saw you, but it wasn't you?"

I nodded.

"Bloody hell...I thought I was losing my mind."

He wasn't the only one. "I have to get rid of her. I thought breaking the curse would do that, but it's only made things worse. It was Laria who pushed me down the stairs...or Randall, who was also a servant at the castle at the same time as Laria."

He went quiet on me. I could see him trying hard to process everything I'd said. His jaw tightened. "Is it possible to kill a ghost, because I'm this close to doing just that from what I've heard."

I smiled. "You and Shane both."

"Shane knows?" He sounded surprised.

"So does Cait, Megan, and Cass. Laria kind of made herself known last night." I didn't get into details. Honestly, it was probably better if he didn't know the extent of the haunting. "Oh, and there's more."

His gaze searched mine.

"When my mom died, I had a lot of guilt about the wreck and everything. When I woke up in the hospital, I was able to see spirits. I couldn't see her, and that really confused me. I started cutting. It was a way to release the frustration I felt inside. I still cut, Kade. I don't want to..."

I could see his gaze shift to my arm, to the scratches there.

"Those are from Laria." I shifted my arm, showing him the scars on the inside of my elbow. "These are self-inflicted. I have some on my legs, too."

"People at school were talking about you cutting."

No surprise there, especially with Dana hanging pictures of a girl cutting on my locker for everyone to see.

"I think there's more people who cut than any of us realize." He took a deep breath, then released it. "I want to help you, Riley. What can I do?"

"Be my friend."

Once again I saw that strange look in his eyes. "I want to be more than friends. I mean, I can't just be your friend."

"I have to end the curse, because I can't go on like this. She's threatening everyone I love, and I've already put my friends in harm's way. I can't ask you to put yourself even more at risk."

"I'm already involved. Don't push me out of your life, Riley. I couldn't stand it."

"I don't want to push you out of my life. I want you."

He reached out and grabbed hold of my face with both hands. "Then let me help you."

Chapter Five

Kade invited me over Sunday for brunch. I wasn't at the castle for five minutes when Cait walked into Kade's room and took me by the hand, telling him she needed to borrow me for a few minutes.

I followed Cait up the stairs to her room.

Madison, Cait and Kade's twelve-year-old cousin who lived with them, sat cross-legged on the rug. Seeing me, she grinned and jumped to her feet. "I'm so happy you're back together with Kade."

I adored Maddy. She had attitude, and it didn't hurt that she could also see the dead, especially Hanway, a ghost who had been living at the castle for centuries. The two had a tight bond.

I gave her a hug. "Thanks, Maddy. I'm happy we're back together, too."

Cait shut the bedroom door behind her.

Maddy sat down on the bed beside me, her gaze skipping to Cait, who had pulled the desk chair close to the bed and took a seat. She leaned in toward Maddy. "We need you to ask Hanway what Laria wants from Riley...or from any of us, for that matter."

I was glad she didn't mention anything about Laria's threat to kill all of us.

Maddy frowned. "I can't just summon him and he appears like a genie."

She could have fooled me. I remember when Randall had shown himself in the dining room, and how Maddy had called for Hanway and he'd been there within seconds. When Ian was here, there had been times I had called to him and he had appeared; and yet other times, like when I'd been locked inside the mausoleum, when he hadn't shown at all.

Maybe one day I would figure out all the complexities of spirits.

"Let me see if I can get him to answer," Maddy said, closing her eyes.

Cait and I shared a look. This twelve-year-old girl blew me away.

I felt a cold chill in the air, but I didn't see Hanway. Apparently Maddy did, though. She glanced toward the far corner of the room. I could tell she was communicating with him, the way her focus stayed there.

I struggled to focus…to see if I could at least hear him.

Maddy watched the corner of the room intently. "He keeps showing me woods."

I swallowed hard.

She closed her eyes and took a deep breath. "I want to go across the river, toward the woods."

Cait frowned. "What does that mean?"

I was reminded of the dream I'd had last night. Before I spoke up and said anything, I wanted to see what else Hanway had to say.

Maddy put her fingers to her temples. "Rumor says she was buried across the river, up on the hillside in the dense brush. They buried her there, forgot about her, and made sure she would never be found."

My breath caught in my throat.

"Does he know where exactly she's buried?" Cait asked.

Maddy shook her head. "Hanway can't leave the castle, so he wasn't able to follow the family and the servants who buried her. He watched from the castle tower, though, and saw them enter the woods beyond the river. Torch light could be seen high up on the hill."

Cait frowned. "Wait, why can't Hanway leave the castle?"

Maddy looked toward Hanway. "He said that some spirits become trapped in a location and there's nothing they can do...but hope one day to be sent to the white light."

Like Ian had been sent to the white light. I had to wonder if maybe Maddy was holding onto Hanway versus helping him to the light. I also wondered if the day came to let him go, if she would.

Maddy glanced at me and I had the feeling she was reading my thoughts.

"How did this whole seeing spirits start for you, Madison?" I asked.

"I had a dream about my great-grandma when I was like three. She came to me the night she died and said she had a stroke. I didn't even know what a stroke was. I told my mom that she had died. When the phone rang an hour later and she learned my grandma had died, she screamed and then watched me close from then on. I started to see a lot of shadows and images out of the corner of my eye, and I always felt like I was being watched."

Maddy cleared her throat. "When I was eight we moved to an apartment in downtown Glasgow. There this little girl would come out of the closet at night and talk to me. She said she lived in the building years before when a fire destroyed it. She didn't make it out."

"That's bloody horrible," Cait said, glancing over her shoulder, like she expected the girl to show up at any second.

"She became my friend," Maddy said absently. "I ran home from school every single day to play with her. Then one day my mum said we were moving. I was so sad. I couldn't imagine not seeing Emma any longer. I never saw her again."

What Maddy didn't say, but I could feel, was that Emma had been her best friend, and she'd lost that best friend and it had left its mark on her.

"Shortly after, my mum dropped me off here and I met Hanway." She hugged her knees to her chest. "It might seem weird to everyone else because he's a man."

"No one thinks it's weird, Maddy," Cait said reassuringly. "Some things happen for a reason." She leaned forward and ruffled Maddy's hair. "He's your friend and you're lucky to have him."

Maddy smiled at Cait. "I *am* lucky."

"Maybe Hanway is why you came to Braemar to begin with," Cait added.

Maddy shrugged. "I doubt my mom's drug addiction has anything to do with a spirit needing me, but thanks for trying to make me feel better."

Cait and I locked eyes and we cracked up. Leave it to Maddy to take a sincere moment and call 'bullshit.'

She frowned at both of us. I felt for Maddy, for being abandoned by both parents, for living in fear of the moment her mother might come knocking on the castle door to take her away to a life of instability and moving from one place to the next. Leaving Hanway and the MacKinnons would be devastating for her, and I hoped more than anything that day never came.

"So do you think Hanway could point toward the burial spot?" I asked, wanting and needing to validate what I had seen in my dream.

Maddy glanced toward Hanway. "He said yes, but we have to go up to the battlements to see."

I followed them out of the room and up the tower steps, my mind racing. What would happen if I did find Laria's grave? Would she get over her anger and frustration toward me and the MacKinnons or would things just continue to escalate?

We headed up another staircase, and then out onto the battlements. "Show me," Maddy said, going up on her tiptoes and looking out over the stone wall.

"He says that it looks a lot different now than it did back then. That tree is in the way," she said motioning to a group of trees. "See the stump off to the right of the tallest oak there?"

I nodded.

"There's a very crude pathway that leads deep into the woods and toward the top of the hill."

My pulse skittered.

"Hanway said the pathway forks off in several different directions when you get about midway up the hillside. Stay to the right, and it will lead you to the very top of the hill."

Cait frowned. "She's buried at the top of the hill?"

Maddy chewed her lower lip and frowned. "Just on the other side of the hill. No one wanted the grave to be found...ever."

"I dreamt about the grave last night," I blurted, and both Cait and Maddy looked at me. "Where Hanway is saying it is, is what I had seen in my dream. In my dream I stood at the top of the hill and looked down at the castle."

Cait turned to me and smiled. "Then that means we're on the right track." She patted Maddy on the back. "Good job, Maddy. Tell Hanway thanks."

Maddy beamed. "You just told him yourself."

"Nice." Cait looked at me, and lifted a brow. "So, when are we going in?"

"Cait, you don't have to go…"

"I want to go, Ri." Cait looked determined. "This is affecting my family too, and I want an end to it."

"You want an end to what?"

We all turned. Kade stood at the doorway watching us.

"An end to Laria's haunting," Cait said in response to his question.

He stepped out onto the battlements, came up behind me, and slid his arms around my waist. "I agree. It's time for this to stop."

I leaned back against his strong chest.

Cait took Maddy by the hand and headed for the door. "Come on, squirt. Let's give these two some space."

"You're not in this alone, you know that, right?" Kade pressed a kiss to the top of my head. "I was serious when I told you I wanted to help you. I don't want to be left out of this. If it affects you, it affects me."

"I'm grateful for your help," I said, staring off at the hillside.

"So…what were you guys doing up here?"

I glanced at him. "Laria is buried up on that hill."

He frowned.

"Apparently that's just one more reason for her to be angry."

"Does she forget that she killed Ian and that's why his family wanted revenge?"

I'm sure she didn't forget what she had done to Ian, or what Ian's family had done to her, for one second.

"But what can you do about her being buried where she's at? Does she expect you to find her body and have it moved?"

"I don't know what she wants, but the grave obviously has something to do with all of it." I turned in his arms. "I don't want to talk about her any more." Honestly, I was so sick of Laria controlling my life. The moments of peace I had were so rare, and I just wanted to be with Kade without looking over my shoulder.

He smiled at me. "How about a motorcycle ride before dinner?"

The motorcycle was of the dirt bike variety. I slid the helmet on that Kade had handed me, and he brushed my hands out of the way to buckle it. The sides of his mouth lifted in a soft smile, and my heart gave a lurch. I liked feeling cared for.

"Are you scared?"

"Not at all," I replied. My family owned dirt bikes that we used at our property in the Columbia River Gorge. Shane and I had spent hours a day on those minibikes, blazing trails through the hundred acres of national forest that backed up to the cedar vacation home where we had spent nearly every weekend during the spring and summer when we were younger.

Sliding a leg over the motorcycle seat, I settled in behind Kade and wrapped my arms around his narrow waist. I liked the intimacy, and as he kicked the engine over and hit first gear we were off.

He started off slowly across the lawn, shifted into second gear, and waved to Maddy and Cait who watched us from the courtyard. The minute we were up over the hill, he hit third and then fourth gear, and we were flying across the green grass, parallel to the river.

Exhilaration rushed through me. I had forgotten this incredible feeling—of the wind against my face, the freedom of being a part of nature, part of the landscape.

A small stone bridge crossed the river ahead of us.

I became nervous that we were headed that way. I didn't trust Laria, and being on that side of the river, and getting closer to the hillside where she'd been buried just made me more uncomfortable.

Thankfully we didn't head up into the hills. In fact, there was a small little track that was just far enough off the road to be invisible from traffic passing by. After a dozen laps, Kade pulled off the track and stopped. He glanced back at me. "You want to go solo?"

It had been years since I'd ridden a bike, so I was a little rusty, but I was also excited. "Sure." I only hoped I didn't make an ass out of myself.

I killed the engine immediately, and when Kade stepped forward to help me out, I put the bike in neutral, flipped out the kick starter with my hand, and putting all my body weight into it, turned the engine over on the first crank.

Kade's lips split into a wide smile. I had surprised him, I knew that, and, in a way, I was surprising myself. It felt incredible.

The first few laps I was a bit wobbly, and I'll admit, I was nervous, especially when I nearly lost control after going a little too fast over one jump.

I had surprised him, I knew that, and, in a way, I was surprising myself. It felt incredible.

On the third lap around, my heart gave a jolt when I noticed what looked like the girl who had been sacrificed from my dream, standing by a tree.

I rode past Kade, who was leaning back on his elbows, legs crossed at the ankle, and grinning from ear to ear.

The girl was there; this time she stepped out from the tree and gestured toward something behind me. I looked over my shoulder, and the entire bike went the same direction. I overcorrected and almost hit the side of another jump. I rounded the corner and started heading back toward Kade, and immediately saw what the girl was referring to.

My stomach dropped to my toes.

Laria, Randall, and the coven were coming up behind Kade.

I pulled back on the throttle and held on, skipping off the track and onto the grass. Big mistake. It was bumpier than the track.

Kade stood up and brushed at his butt, and a scream froze in my throat when Randall came up right behind him.

The witches made like a wall behind Randall. I gunned it even more, knowing I was pushing it.

Kade's eyes were wide when I pulled up beside him and killed the engine. "Wow, you constantly surprise me."

I heard the pride in his voice, and yet I couldn't savor the small victory, not when we were surrounded by the enemy.

"We will kill him and all that you hold dear," Laria said, coming up from beside Kade, sliding a hand over his shoulder, down his bicep, to rest on his hand.

Kade brushed at his arm, like an insect had landed on him.

He actually felt her...

"I don't understand what you want from me," I said, speaking in my mind. *"I don't get it. Why not just let it go. Ian is gone. Kade is here, but we're alive. You're not."*

Laria hovered above the ground a good six inches, and then even higher. I know she tried to intimidate me, and quite frankly, she was doing a pretty damn good job, especially surrounded by Randall and the coven.

For the first time, I got a look at the faces of some of the others. They ranged from my age to like sixty. I was stunned that they were all against me. How could so many people I had never met before hate me so much? What had I ever done to them, aside from help

Ian cross over?

"Do you trust me?" I asked Kade.

He frowned. "Of course. Why…"

"We need to go *right* now."

His eyes widened. "They're here?"

I nodded.

"What do they want?"

"Me."

He grabbed my hand, thrust his helmet on, and seconds later we were on the bike and flying across the field.

I held onto him tightly, and I could feel the pounding of his heart against my chest. I have no idea how they were able to do it, but they were moving with us, many just a blur.

Screams tore through the quiet, drowning out the sound of the motorcycle.

Fingernails dug into the skin on my back. When the castle came into view, I breathed a sigh of relief.

I buried my face into Kade's back, praying for help.

Laria's threat that she would kill Kade and all I held dear rang in my ears. What next? If something happened to him, my family, or my friends, I'd never forgive myself.

My arms tightened around Kade.

We caught air over the last hill before the castle lawn. Cait and Maddy had been sitting in the courtyard, and came running out.

I thought for a second Kade might have lost the brakes until he came to a stop a few feet from the courtyard wall. I slid off the bike and removed my helmet. He was off, putting the kick-stand up and removing his helmet.

"What happened to your shirt?" Maddy asked.

I glanced over my shoulder. My blouse was torn from the very bottom to just above my bra line.

Kade's jaw clenched. "What the hell? When did that happen?"

"A few minutes ago."

Cait lifted the shirt. "Riley, you have scratch marks all the way down your spine."

Kade threw his helmet on the grass and looked at my back. "This is too much." He looked in the direction we had just come. "You bloody cowards, why go after a girl who can't fight you? You touch her again, and I'll make sure you spend the rest of your days in hell."

I really wish he hadn't said that. Threatening this group of spirits could blow up in all of our faces.

Chapter Six

Wade had dropped me off at the inn and made me promise to call if there were any other attacks. I didn't dare tell him everything that had happened to me so far, especially since he'd been so quiet ever since seeing the scratches on my back. I already knew how tough it was for everyone to understand just how bad things had gotten.

Cait had let me borrow a shirt, and I'd tossed my blouse on the fire in the dining room, watching it go up in smoke. It figures Laria would mess up one of my favorite shirts. I changed into my pajamas and went straight to bed.

Dad popped his head in, told me goodnight, and mentioned that he was heading to Edinburgh in the morning.

He was running to his girlfriend again. Being with us for days on end had probably been family overload for him. For all I knew, he could have a drawer at Cheryl's house where he kept his things. "That's fine," I murmured, wishing I could be a bit more like Shane—to where my dad taking up with another woman didn't bother me so much. I knew he would have to move on sooner or later, and I wanted him to have companionship, but I just wished he could have waited a while.

But as I was learning—shit happens, and sometimes all you could do was hang on for the ride.

Kind of like the ride Laria was taking me on. A terrifying ride that was testing my patience and my sanity.

I browsed every book I had on psychic gifts that Anne Marie and Miss Akin had given me, but nowhere did any of them mention what to do—aside from protection rituals that I'd already used—to get rid of a spirit. One positive thing about Dad leaving for the week was it would give me some time to at least use the internet and search for information without him looking over my shoulder. I'd also ask Megan to search for books on hauntings and ghosts at the library where she worked.

The last time I looked at the alarm clock it said three thirty three. When I woke up a few hours later, I felt like I'd slept for thirty minutes.

I took a long shower, even turning on the cold water to wake myself up a bit more. Dressed in skinny jeans, boots, and a lightweight sweater, I opened my bedroom door.

Miss A was walking by with a basket of laundry on her hip. "Good morning, love. There's some toast on a plate for you."

"Thanks, Miss A."

She grinned and continued down the hall, toward my dad's room. The door was wide open, so either he had left or he was downstairs in his study or the kitchen.

I walked into the kitchen. Dad was there, pouring himself a cup of coffee. He grabbed three packets of his favorite sweetener, opened them, and dumped them in. "I'll be home sometime this weekend. Be sure to call if you need anything."

I knew the drill. I nodded, hating the awkwardness between us.

"Are you okay?" he asked, his brows furrowed.

"Yeah, I'm fine," I said, picking up the piece of toast and taking a bite.

His phone rang. He glanced at the screen and immediately walked out of the room.

Toast in hand, I walked outside, onto the back porch. I looked toward the castle, and more specifically, the hill where Laria was buried. The place where countless sacrifices had gone down. I had seen the girl who had been sacrificed in my dreams last night. I wished she could have told me what she wanted. I kept recalling her repeated warning...*Find her, and you find them all.*

"What are you doing?"

I jumped, and turned to find Shane. His hair was still wet, curling at the collar of his well-worn T-shirt.

"I had a dream about Laria's grave the other night."

His eyes widened a little and he stepped out onto the porch, shutting the door behind him. "Where is it?"

I knew my brother too well. If I told him exactly where the grave was, he'd go on his own or with Milo and Richie and try to confront Laria and the others, which would only make matters worse for all of us. "It's up on that hill somewhere."

"You go alone, and I swear to God I'll kick your ass, understand?" Shane said, sounding more like our dad by the day.

I gave him a salute. "Got it."

"What if you do find the grave...then what?"

"I don't know yet. I just feel like I have to go there. Like I'm being drawn there. With Dad leaving, I'll have time to actually browse websites. I hope that maybe something will surface that can help us."

"Well, anything's worth a shot at this point," he said, taking a bite out of an apple. "I say we take our friends with us. Safety in numbers and all that."

For some reason I couldn't imagine some of our friends going on a ghost hunt in the woods.

"You think Richie and Milo would go?"

Shane nodded. "I think so, if I tell them I need them."

I seriously doubted Megan and Cass would be up for it, even if I told them I needed them, but I'd ask them all the same. "When do you want to go?"

"We need daylight, because the last thing we need is to get lost in the woods at night. So it has to be on a weekend."

I couldn't imagine not having Shane to talk to now. "Thanks for being here for me."

His brows furrowed and his lips quirked. "I'm your brother. I'll always be there for you."

"Do your friends know about the haunting?"

"I have a feeling Megan has spilled to Milo, especially since he's been asking me questions about ghosts, a subject that was never brought up before."

I finished off the toast and licked the butter off my fingers. "They probably think we're crazy."

"Speak for yourself." He laughed under his breath. "Plus, if your friends don't think you're crazy, then I doubt mine will feel differently. And knowing Cass, she's probably already run her mouth and they all know anyway."

True.

He lifted his brows. "If they do give me shit, then maybe I need to invite them over for a little impromptu Ouija board session."

My stomach tightened. "I thought you got rid of it?"

He winked. "Just messing with you."

I stopped myself short of asking him what exactly he'd done

with the board, but honestly, I didn't need to know. Just as long as it didn't magically appear, I was fine with it.

"By the way, you handled yourself really well with your friends the night of the sleepover."

I smiled. "Thanks, I tried. I know it's not easy to hear, but I give them credit for staying around after hearing everything." I pressed my lips together. "I told them about the cutting, too."

He didn't look surprised, which made me wonder if Cait had said something to him. It didn't matter. The truth was out there, and I was at peace with everyone knowing.

"Cait has your back, but I think you know that."

I did know it, and when it came to the supernatural, Cait seemed to have a better grasp on it than the others. Plus, she didn't seem to be as afraid. "You like her a lot, don't you?"

He nodded. "She's fun to be around. Do you mind if I see her?"

I shook my head. "No. She's a sweetheart, and I know she really likes you. I'm just curious—what happened to Joni?" When we had first moved to Braemar, Shane had started hanging out with Joni, a Emo girl who seemed as into Shane as he was her. Things had changed though when Laria had started possessing him.

His jaw tightened, and a nerve ticked in his jaw. "I heard through the grapevine she had a long-term boyfriend in Glasgow."

That surprised me, especially since Joni seemed to genuinely like Shane. "Sorry." At least I knew that Laria hadn't destroyed that relationship.

"Yeah, well, it is what it is. I like her, I do...but I'm not touching that one. I wouldn't want the same thing to happen to me."

"Bad karma."

He nodded. "Right. No thanks. What about you and Kade? Cait said you'd patched things up."

Shane had really defended me when all the stuff about Dana and Kade came to light. "Yeah, we did. We're really good."

"That's gr—"

"Are you trying to be late for school?" Dad asked, startling both me and Shane. I hadn't even heard the door open. He made a show of checking the time on his watch. "It's quarter after."

We had less than fifteen minutes to get to school.

"We're headed out now," Shane said, ducking past him. "See ya this weekend!"

Miss Akin handed Shane a breakfast sandwich and me a glass of milk. I chugged it and raced upstairs to brush my teeth and grab my backpack.

Shane met me at the front door.

"I'll see you two at the end of the week," Dad said, waving to us. "Friday, or maybe even Saturday, depending on my work load."

"Work load, my ass," Shane said under his breath.

There was no mention of calling us every night or wishing Shane good luck with his football game. How quickly things had changed.

"Later," Shane said, sliding his backpack onto his shoulder, and I waved to Dad before we crossed the road.

We had just passed over the bridge into town when I felt like we were being followed. I glanced over my shoulder and didn't see anyone, except two 'tween girls who had their heads together and were giggling as the one read something from a book.

I smiled to myself, remembering when Becca, my former best friend since elementary school, and I would do the same.

The strange sensation of being followed and watched continued. By the time I turned and looked again, Shane asked. "What are you feeling?"

"There's someone following us."

He scanned the area. "Yeah, two girls."

"No, there's a spirit."

"Can you tell who it is?"

I shook my head. "Not yet."

The girls walked into the market. The feelings grew stronger.

"Come on, we have to pick it up if we're not going to be late."

We passed by the post office and I glanced at our reflections in the window. My pulse skittered when across the street I saw a girl standing on the sidewalk, facing us.

It was the blonde ghost from the dream. The sacrifice.

I glanced over and she was gone.

I didn't start to relax until I saw the school, or actually Kade's Range Rover sitting in the parking lot. Shane seemed to relax, too.

We parted ways in the courtyard. "Text me if you need anything," he said. "I'll check my cell phone during class breaks."

"Sounds good. I'll see you tonight after football practice."

"See you then."

When I entered the hallway, Cass was standing at her locker, energy drink in hand. She had large black circles beneath her eyes.

My stomach clenched. I had a horrible suspicion that Laria was the reason behind how tired Cass appeared. "You look exhausted."

"I am," she said, pushing a shaky hand through her hair. "I couldn't sleep for shit all weekend. I kept thinking about you being yanked under the bed. I talked to Megan and she's having some pretty freaky dreams. I'm really concerned about her. I haven't seen her this morning and she's not picking up her phone."

I felt sick with guilt. My friends were going through hell because of me, and I was afraid things were only going to get worse for all of us.

Come to think of it, I hadn't heard from Megan at all since she'd left my house Saturday afternoon.

Cass slid a thumb under her backpack strap. "Megan dreamt about Laria at your house the night of the slumber party."

"Is she sure it was Laria?"

Cass nodded. "Yeah, she said she had the same brown hair, dark eyes, and even the same green gown Laria had been wearing the day we saw her on the roadside on the way home from Aberdeen."

No wonder Megan had been so quiet at breakfast. I wished she would have said something to me about the dream.

"Then she dreamt about Laria on Saturday night and again last night." Cass glanced over her shoulder to make sure no one was listening. "She said when she wakes up she feels like she's being held down. No matter how hard she tries to move, she can't."

It sounded just like what Shane had been through, and Anne Marie had mentioned dreaming of Laria after the séance we'd had with Miss Akin. And now Anne Marie was dead.

"You're not having dreams?" I asked, holding my breath as I waited for her to answer.

Cass shook her head. "I popped one of Bitchzilla's sleeping pills last night because I couldn't turn my brain off after talking to Megan about her nightmares. I didn't have any dreams, but I feel all groggy this morning, kind of like I'm in a fog. Not good, especially since I have a chemistry test this morning."

This was too much. My friends' lives were being affected by something they had no control over. I really hated the idea that Cass was taking her step mother's sleeping pills.

From the corner of my eye I saw someone standing toward the end of the hall, watching me. I glanced up and my pulse skittered. Peter lounged against the tile wall. When I looked at him, he pushed away from the wall and waved at me.

Laria was unbelievable. Did she forget she had told me she was masquerading as Peter during the Ouija board session Friday night?

I abruptly looked away.

Riley! He yelled, like you would do if a friend was trying to gain your attention.

Wow, really? Did she seriously believe I was going to fall for this?

The warning bell for first period rang and Cass cussed under her breath and chugged the rest of her energy drink.

"I'll see you at lunch, okay?"

I wish I'd gotten to school a little earlier, so at least I would have seen Kade before class started. As it was, I entered first period right as the bell rang. I was the only one who wasn't in their seat. I almost didn't recognize Dana, whose red hair had been bleached to an unflattering cat pee yellow.

I bit back a smile. Still, crappy bleach job and all, she watched me with a smug smile that didn't quite reach her narrowed eyes.

Aaron, the guy known as "violin boy" was also a cutter, and he'd always been nice to me. He flashed a toothy grin when he saw me. "Hey, Riley."

"Hey," I said, quickly taking my seat while ignoring Mr. Monahan's icy stare. He expected students to be in their seats when the bell rang.

"I heard about the wreck," Aaron whispered. "You okay?"

Thankfully Mr. Monahan was too busy writing our assignment on the board to pay any attention.

"We're both fine. Technically, it wasn't a wreck. I mean, we took out a fence, but it looked worse than it—"

"Mr. Johnson and Miss Williams, please do not socialize on my time," Mr. Monahan said in a clipped tone, putting the chalk down.

Everyone giggled, and Mr. Monahan clapped his hands together twice and snapped, "Enough!"

Shaking his head in disgust, he lifted his clipboard and began to take roll, the sound of his pencil making a scraping sound against the paper as he checked each name off.

Peter was suddenly standing beside my desk, an inch away. Startled, I nearly jumped out of my chair. The kid right next to me lifted his brows.

I shifted in my seat, and tried to settle my nerves. This was going to be a very long day, especially if Peter, or Laria, was going to constantly try to get my attention.

Ignoring the strange looks directed at me by my classmates, I stared straight ahead and didn't let on that I could see Peter.

Peter waved his hand in front of my face. I didn't blink. I guess there was a part of me that didn't want to look him in the eye and suddenly see Laria there. Why hadn't I caught on before? I needed to be careful with who I trusted, especially anyone in the spirit world... kind of like the blonde woman from the witchcraft sacrifice who was showing up lately.

"What's wrong with you?" Peter asked.

I reached down, grabbed my backpack, and unloaded my textbook and notebook paper.

"Did I do something to make you mad at me?" There was no ignoring the desperation in his voice. Laria was good; I'd give her that. Extremely convincing.

"I don't understand," he said, almost to himself. He reached out, put his hand over mine and squeezed. It took everything within me not to look at him. Why didn't I have that dark feeling whenever Laria was around? Wouldn't I feel something that made me think it was her? Even when she'd masqueraded as my mom, I'd felt something was off. All I felt now was sadness...and that's exactly what

Laria wanted. For me to be as miserable as she was.

Mr. Monahan opened the classroom door and walked into the hall to place the roll sheet into the box for the office aide to collect. Through the small window in the door, I saw him talking to the attendance secretary.

Peter sighed heavily and walked to the far side of the room, sitting on the table where I'd first seen him. His gaze drilled into me, like he was almost daring me to look at him.

"Do you want to come over sometime?" Aaron asked me, and I looked up, surprised. It had been so quiet in the room, that others had heard us.

"Go, Aaron," a guy in the back row said.

Dana, or one of her friends must have heard too, because she was cracking up. She leaned over and whispered in her friend's ear. They both laughed and glanced back at me.

Aaron obviously didn't know that Kade and I were back together. Actually, no one aside from friends and family knew, but soon they would. I didn't want to shut Aaron down in front of everyone because I hoped we could be friends.

Aaron shifted in his chair. "I thought you might want to see my puppy."

"Yeah, puppy as in cock," I heard Dana say under her breath.

"You are such a bitch." The words were out of my mouth before I could stop them. Everyone turned to stare at me, their gazes shifting back and forth between me and Dana, like they were expecting me to leap out of my chair and attack her.

Though I was tempted, I stayed in my seat. Dana was completely twisted around in her chair, staring at me, her eyes mere slits. "What did you say?"

"I called you a bitch," I replied, not backing down.

Dana lifted a penciled-in brow. "You're just pissed because you couldn't keep your boyfriend satisfied and he had to come to me."

More than one person in the room gasped.

In my peripheral vision, Peter stood up. Now was *not* the time for Laria to taunt me.

"Dana, you spread your legs for anyone," Aaron said, and at the most inopportune time—when Mr. Monahan was walking back into the room.

His brows lifted to his receding hairline. "Did you say something, Mr. Johnson?"

Aaron sank back in his chair.

I felt horrible. The last thing I wanted was to get Aaron in trouble. He was a sweet guy, and he'd probably never been in trouble a day in his life.

"Mr. Johnson, may I have a word with you out in the hall?" Mr. Monahan said.

Shit. I chewed on my thumb nail, mad at myself for responding to Dana to begin with. She had managed to get under my skin.

Aaron sighed heavily and grabbed his backpack.

"Leave it," Mr. Monahan barked.

The backpack slid to the floor. Aaron swallowed hard, glanced at me, and followed Mr. Monahan out the door.

Dana looked over her shoulder. "Looks like you got your new boyfriend in trouble," she said, just above a whisper.

"Why don't you shut up," the quiet boy who sat to my right, said, surprising everyone, especially me. He never said too much to me.

"Fuck off, fatty," Dana quipped. She opened her mouth to say something else when Peter ran his fingers down the length of the chalkboard. Surprisingly, everyone heard it. On the chalkboard, there were nail marks.

"What the hell?" a girl said behind me. "Where did those lines come from?"

Dana made a reference that I was telekinetic like the girl from the movie Carrie, and that I had made the noise and marks while remaining seated.

Mr. Monahan walked back into the room with Aaron on his heels. Two bright blotches of color stained Aaron's cheeks. He glanced at me, and ever so slowly the corners of his mouth lifted slightly.

I breathed a sigh of relief. Aaron's sterling reputation must have kept him from visiting the principal's office.

Mr. Monahan cleared his throat in exaggerated fashion. "I want to make myself abundantly clear to every last one of you. I do not want to hear one more negative exchange of words in this classroom. Is that understood?"

"Yes, Mr. Monahan," everyone said...except for me.

Mr. Monahan skewered me with his gaze. He had the art of intimidation down.

I nodded and he looked down at his desk. "All right, now that we've wasted ten minutes, please open your textbooks to page forty-two."

I opened my book and watched Peter from the corner of my eye. He sat on the desk, legs kicking back and forth, just like a kid would do. Why would Laria draw attention away from the argument I'd been having with Dana? Wouldn't she have enjoyed it and even egged it on?

That question would continue to eat at me for the rest of the morning.

Chapter Seven

Throughout the day Peter tried to get my attention, event putting his face right up to mine during Science. I didn't miss a beat and pretended to look right through him.

Laria played the part of an innocent eleven-year-old boy well. "Peter" genuinely seemed wounded by my lack of attention, and he was nearly screaming at me to notice him.

Misgivings ate away at me. What if I were wrong? What if Peter really was an eleven-year-old boy who had desperately been seeking someone to talk to? What if Laria wanted me to believe that she was Peter?

I was so confused, and conflicted. Although it was tough, I ignored him. By the time lunch came around, I was ready for a distraction.

"Were you late this morning?" Kade asked, as he slid onto the bench beside me.

I hadn't seen him when I came into the cafeteria. As usual, he looked gorgeous and my heart swelled.

"Yeah, I was late."

"I thought so. I looked for you. I called once and even texted."

I slid my phone out of my pocket and flipped to my messages. "I didn't get a call or a text from you."

He removed his phone from his pocket. "I swear I called and texted you."

"Sure you did," I said teasingly.

He didn't return the smile. "Seriously, I texted you. I was worried, especially with everything that's going on."

I was touched by his concern, and more than a little bothered that the phone messages weren't registering on either one of our phones.

He frowned. "I called from my car, and then texted before the bell rang."

"I got a late start. My dad left for Edinburgh this morning..."

The missing phone and text messages were suddenly forgotten. His eyes lit up, a smile tugging at the edges of his lips.

The blood in my veins turned warm. I knew that look. I grinned and shook my head.

"I almost called you late last night, but it was too late," he said, becoming serious again. "I had been online researching hauntings, and I came across a video clip of a family who had been dealing with the spirit possession of their son. The boy was being scratched; he was acting out of character—depressed, angry, and saying things that didn't make sense. His mum said he was even using a different vocabulary, words he wasn't even familiar with. He essentially became someone else."

"What did they do?" I asked.

Across the table, Cait and Cass had stopped eating and were listening intently.

"The family brought in a ghost hunting team and they discovered the spirit haunting the boy was a man who had lived on the property before, and he was buried in a nearby cemetery. They then called in a specialist to do a binding ceremony. This lady, along with the boy's parents, went to the man's grave, drove a nail into the ground, and told the spirit it was anchored to that place and was no longer allowed to bother the family again. She then said a blessing over the grave."

"Did it work?" Cass asked.

Kade nodded. "Yeah. The family says the boy was fine after that."

"Then that's what we'll do," I said. "I was hoping we could make a trek up to the grave on Saturday. Shane said he'd ask his friends along, too."

"Of course I'll come with you. I wouldn't let you go without me," Kade said, squeezing my hand.

Cait and Cassie looked past my shoulder and frowned.

I turned to see what had caught their attention. Megan walked toward our table, and I was stunned by her appearance. Her auburn hair was pulled up in a sloppy ponytail, she had little to no makeup on, and deep, dark half circles bracketed her brown eyes.

"Are you all right, Meg?" I asked.

She shook her head. "No."

"I'll let you girls talk, all right?" Kade said. "Can I see you tonight?"

I glanced at Megan. Although I wanted to spend time with Kade, I could tell my friend was hurting, and since it was my fault she was suffering, I needed to be there for her. "We'll see, okay? Give me a call after practice."

"Will do." He leaned forward, gave me a kiss, and went to sit with his friends.

Cait came around the table and sat in the place Kade had vacated. "Wow, you look like shit, Meg."

"That bitch is haunting my dreams," Megan said, glancing at the group to our right, who was looking our way.

"Do you mind?" Cass said.

The group of girls abruptly looked away.

Mean-mugging them, Cass shifted so her back was to them and Megan was hidden from view.

"She's going to kill me, I swear," Megan said, scratching her forehead. "I can't have this. I mean, what if she starts haunting my little brother? He's so young...and this could mess him up for life."

I completely understood her concern, especially after the story Kade had just told us about the boy.

I'd never forgive myself if that happened to Megan's little brother.

"I have no peace. I'm constantly on edge, and it's like she knows that I know that she's there." Tears welled in Megan's eyes, but she blinked them back before they spilled over. "I'm so tired."

Cait glanced at me, eyes wide.

I swallowed past the tightness in my throat. "I'm so sorry, Megan. I wish—"

"You can't help it, Ri," Cait said, squeezing my shoulder. "It's not your fault. You're as much of a victim as anyone, if not more so."

"I give you credit," Megan said, looking at me dead in the eyes. "I couldn't deal with it as long as you have. I feel like I'm coming undone, and the dreams are wicked." She lowered her voice. "That bitch is relentless, I tell you. I try to wake up from the nightmare, but it's like she's keeping me in that state right before you wake. It's almost like I'm watching myself dream, if that makes sense, and I'm watching her and feeling her holding me down. When I do actually wake up, I find I can't move at all. I want to scream, but I can't even breathe."

What she was saying nearly mirrored what Shane had told me about his dreams when we'd first moved to Braemar. I knew the horror of having Laria show up in nightmares, and when you woke up it was tough to shake it. I could see the physical and emotional strain it was putting on Megan, which gave me even more incentive to end the haunting once and for all.

At least now I could look into binding spirits.

Milo came up from behind Megan and embraced her. "How are you feelin', love?"

"What are you doing here?" Megan asked, looking really happy to see him. "How did you get out of study hall?"

He shrugged. "If my girl needs me, a little thing like class won't stop me from seeing her."

Leaning her head against his shoulder, she sighed. "I feel like shit. I just want to go home and sleep."

For once Milo was completely serious. He brushed his thumb along her jaw and kissed her softly. "How about I come over and we'll take a nice long nap. Get rid of these circles beneath your eyes."

Megan pouted. "Sounds incredible, but unfortunately I have to work today."

"Blow it off," Milo said, his voice stern. "You need to take care of yourself or you're going to be sick if you keep this up. If it's about the money you'll lose by not working, then I'll pay you to stay with me."

"Isn't that like prostitution?" Cass teased, a hint of a smile on her lips. At least she was trying to find the humor in a horrible situation.

Milo shook his head.

Megan chewed her lower lip. "Maybe I'll see if Kelsey can cover for me. I know she's looking for more hours. Will you help me find her? I think she has this lunch."

"Definitely." Milo looked relieved as he helped her up.

As they walked off, Cass stood. "I'll be right back."

We watched as she walked toward Johan's table.

Cait pushed her uneaten salad away from her. "How about we take a walk in the woods this afternoon?"

My gut clenched. "Shane and Kade would kill us if we went without them." They both had football practice every day after school, which meant the first opportunity for them to go with us would be the weekend.

"I'm not trying to be a bitch, Ri, but does Megan *look* like she can wait until this weekend?"

She had a point.

I shook my head. "No." As terrified as I was to go to Laria's grave without an entourage, I was even more terrified at what could possibly happen to my friends if I waited. Dreams of being held down and being tormented would only escalate. If Laria started scratching and choking my friends, it was only a matter of time before she succeeded in following through on her threat to kill us all.

"I just don't see where we have a choice. Like Megan said, what if Laria starts tormenting her little brother? Then who's next? I don't want to sound selfish, but I honestly don't want it to be me, and yet I know it's a matter of time, especially if we don't try to stop her now. Let's face it, Cass has already admitted to popping sleeping pills, and that's just dangerous."

It was dangerous to take pills. As dangerous as it was for me to confront a malevolent spirit.

"All right, I'll go," I said, not wanting to think about what would happen when Shane found out I was going to Laria's grave without him.

Cait didn't mess around. By the time I met her behind the cemetery, she looked ready for a hike into the Andes mountains. She wore a bandana over her head, cargo pants, hiking boots, and a fleece vest over her long-sleeved shirt. I'd bet my life she had as much survivor gear shoved into her stuffed backpack as she could fit.

At least someone knew what they were doing.

I felt like an amateur with my jeans, tennis shoes, and lightweight flannel. At least I'd thought to bring a jacket in my pack for later... just in case, along with the nail, hammer, and the paper where I'd written down the words from the video Kade had been talking about. The lady binding the grave had been short and to the point.

I also brought a flashlight, extra batteries, water bottle, and a couple of protein bars.

"Okay, we don't want to lose each other. If we do...we have these," she said, handing me a Hello Kitty walkie-talkie.

I tried to hide my smile but failed. "Hello Kitty..."

"A phase I was going through. They work, though. I tested them out with Maddy."

"Maddy knows we're going?"

"Hell, no. She'd freak out and probably tell Mum." Cait added another water bottle to my pack. "Just in case. We want to be sure we stay hydrated."

"We're just heading to the top of that hill."

Her lips quirked. "The top of that hill is miles away, Ri. I know that it looks like it would be a quick sprint, but honestly, it's much further than it looks, and the terrain can be a bit dodgy at times."

Not the most comforting of words, especially with the afternoon sun beating down on us.

"Let's get moving," she said, and we started off at a clip, both of us excited and nervous as we made our way into the woods. It wasn't too far in when the pathways started veering off in different directions...just as Hanway had told Maddy.

At first, Cait used the compass on her iPhone to track direction, but soon the phone dropped out of range, and there was no signal. That made me nervous. If we got into trouble, we were shit out of luck.

Cait was obviously in better shape than I was, because she hiked about ten steps ahead of me. Every once in a while she would wait, but inevitably she'd pull ahead again.

I knew it was wrong of me to do, but I wanted to be distracted, and I wanted to know what Cait was thinking. Out of all my friends, she was the toughest one to figure out.

What I didn't expect were thoughts of my brother, mostly the two of them making out and rolling around on his bed. Apparently they had done more than just sleep at the slumber party. I quickly pushed the thought away before I "saw" more than I wanted to.

"Our brothers would kill us if they knew what we were doing," I said, speaking my fears aloud.

She glanced back at me and grinned. "What they don't know won't hurt them. And I'm sure as hell not saying anything to either one of them. Let's just hope we're successful, we bind the grave, and we return home and our lives become peaceful again."

I hoped she was right. I needed peace. Scratch that, we all needed peace.

"He likes you...a lot. I can tell."

"Really?" She slowed down, and fell into step beside me. "Has he said anything?"

"Yeah, he asked me if I had a problem with him seeing you."

She actually looked nervous. "And what did you say?"

"Do you seriously have to ask me that?" I said, surprised. "I kind of have a thing for your brother, too, you know? I'm assuming you don't care that I'm seeing Kade, so why would I feel weird about you seeing Shane?"

She grinned, obviously relieved. "We're still sort of friends. I was relieved to hear about Joni and her boyfriend, though. I thought maybe I didn't stand a chance in hell, especially since she's so cute. He seemed really into her."

I wasn't about to bring up Joni's boyfriend since I didn't know how much Shane had revealed to his friends. "Have you looked in the mirror?" I asked, and she nudged me and shook her head.

Cait was definitely one of those girls who didn't realize just how gorgeous she was, and I found that refreshing. I'm sure Shane did, too.

I tripped over a tree root. The branches became so thick that they were hiding any sunlight from view, and I didn't know if it was just my imagination, but I swore I heard movement behind us.

Cait glanced at me, some of her bravado fleeing. "I'm sure it's just an animal."

That was hardly reassuring. I hadn't given any thought to animals until now. I'd been too terrified of supernatural beings to worry about anything in the living realm.

"I brought a knife," she said, reaching into the side pocket of her cargo pants. It was a pocketknife, and she flicked a button, exposing a long, shiny blade.

My eyes widened. I didn't know if a knife would be any help with Laria or any other ghost, but I'm sure it would come in handy if we came across an animal.

"How much further do you think?"

"Probably about an hour."

An hour! Oh my God.

I distinctly heard footsteps behind me, running up on us. I stopped and turned, expecting someone to be there.

Cait swallowed hard. Her gaze told me she had heard it, too.

I saw a black figure move from one tree to the next, and then another flash, and yet another dark figure. The same hooded figures I'd seen before.

"They're here," I said, trying to slow my racing heart.

Cait's eyes widened. Suddenly this wasn't so exciting anymore.

"Riiiilllleeeyyyyy," I heard in my ear.

I felt like I'd walked through a thick batch of cobwebs. I wiped at my face and Cait looked at me. "What's wrong?"

"Nothing. I must have walked into a spiderweb or something."

The figures in the woods stopped, and then simultaneously they all turned to face me. I reached out and grabbed Cait's hand. "We're so screwed," I said under my breath.

Her eyes widened. "Where are they?"

A dark, depressing feeling rushed through me. We were completely surrounded. "All around us."

I tried not to panic as icy fingers slid around the back of my neck.

"You will leave here and you shall never return," Laria whispered. I felt a burning sensation where her lips had touched the edge of my ear.

"She's telling us to leave and never return."

Cait stiffened her spine. "Where is she?"

"Beside me."

"Leave her alone," Cait said, staring off to my left. "Leave all of us alone. You are dead."

Laria was well aware she was dead, but I didn't tell Cait that.

"She's on the other side," I said, and Cait's gaze shifted to my right shoulder.

Laria's nails bit into my shoulder. I gritted my teeth against the pain.

"Mom, help us," I said, under my breath.

Laria's laughter echoed in my mind. She was mocking me.

Chill bumps raced up my back, along my spine, and made the hair on my arms stand on end.

I took hold of Cait's hand. "I ask for God and the angels to surround us, to protect us from evil."

Cait repeated my words over and over again, her voice ringing with conviction.

Laria turned from me toward Cait, a slow smile spreading over her lips. She reached out and grabbed hold of her.

At first it was like Cait didn't feel anything, until Laria's fingers slid around her neck and squeezed.

Cait's eyes widened in alarm, and then she looked at me in desperation, asking me without words to do something. Anything.

I pushed Laria hard, and she didn't budge. "Get off her!" I yelled.

From the crowd of cloaked figures, a tall man stepped forward. He pushed the cowl back off his head.

"Oh my God," Cait said, and it was obvious by the terrified expression that she could see Randall as plainly as I did.

Randall flew at me, so fast I didn't have time to move. The breath left me in a rush, and I was slammed against a tree trunk, my face pushed up against the bark. Randall's hand tightened around the back of my neck and squeezed hard. A wave of dizziness washed over me.

Cait screamed so loud it nearly pierced my eardrums. Abruptly the spirits disappeared.

Kade came rushing out of the trees with Shane on his heels. They both looked wildly about. "What's going on?"

Cait was pure white and trembling. All her bravado had gone out the window. I knew how shocking it was to see a spirit, and I have no doubt she had seen Randall. Maybe she'd even seen Laria and the others.

Kade helped me up, and Shane stared daggers at me. "You said you wouldn't come without me."

"How did you know we were here?" I asked sheepishly.

"Maddy showed up at practice," Kade said, brushing the dirt off my back, and looking over his shoulder he scanned the area. "She was freaking out, saying you were in danger, and she told us you had gone in search of Laria's grave."

Shane planted his hands on his hips. "I told you not to come without me." It was really obvious he wasn't about to let it drop. He glanced at Cait. "And what were you thinking?"

"It was my idea," Cait said, and Kade turned to her, surprise on his face.

"Laria is haunting Megan. I mean, you saw her. She looked like shit. I thought we could end it by binding the grave like you mentioned," she said, glancing at Kade. "I just want this to be over for everybody, especially Riley. Christ, how much can one person take?"

Kade brushed a hand over his jaw. "I know you meant well, but this was stupid. I don't know what happened, what the screams were about, but it was obvious you're both terrified, because I've never seen either of you this pale."

"We'd better head back," I said, feeling like we had gone through enough today. Shane was right—the next time we came up, we needed to be prepared.

Kade's fingers threaded through mine. "Promise me you'll never do this again." His gaze shifted to his sister. "That means you, too."

Cait nodded. "I swear I'll wait until we can all go together as a group." Her throat convulsed as she swallowed hard. "Or maybe we should continue. Another hour and we'd be at the top."

Kade looked at Cait. "I'm sure Maddy has said something to Mum by now, which means Dad will be headed this way very soon."

Point taken. The last thing I wanted or needed were Kade and Cait's parents involved. As it was, Kade would have to come up with some excuse why he had missed practice.

Without further argument, we headed back down the hill. We hadn't gone twenty feet when I swore I heard a woman crying. In my mind's eye, I saw an image of the blonde-haired woman who had been sacrificed in these woods.

The gut-wrenching sob made me want to turn around and continue up the hill...but it was obvious by what Cait and I had just experienced that Laria, Randall, and the others were not going to back down without a fight.

We needed to be prepared.

Chapter Eight

Ever since we returned from the hill, I'd felt a presence with me. I couldn't say if it was Laria, Randall, or even the girl who had been sacrificed...but the spirit lingered, staying in the shadows, which was out of character for the malevolent ghost who had taken such pleasure in tormenting me.

Or maybe this was just Laria's way of toying with me—and staying in the dark was the best way to do that.

I couldn't lie still. I'd been staring at the ceiling for the past two hours, looking at the pattern the bedside lamp cast upon the plaster, while listening to the sounds of the house, waiting for someone to come out of the woodwork...but as the seconds ticked away into minutes, the silence became deafening. My legs were restless and adrenaline raced through my body, which was strange, because I was exhausted, both mentally and physically.

I am liquid fire in your veins.

My heart missed a beat. Had I only just imagined the words? I wondered, when suddenly it came again...

The Departed

I am liquid fire in your veins.

I smashed the pillow over my head. The words were as clear as day, coming at me from all sides.

Do you feel me?

Suddenly, dark images raced through my mind—of a group of men dragging a woman out of a barn and into the woods, torches lighting the way. The woman struggled as she was pulled out into the cold, pitch-black night.

There were so many young women screaming now, their faces so close to mine their features were a blur. A sense of overwhelming sadness, fear, and fury came over me, nearly choking me with its intensity.

I had felt emotion before, but this was at a different level altogether. I felt rage within me, and was shocked when tears rolled down my face. Despair, similar to that when I lost my mom, gripped me.

If I started talking, the spirits might never leave. I swallowed past the lump in my throat, threw the covers off my legs, and sat cross-legged on my bed. I was afraid if I let my legs hang over the side of the bed, Laria would rip me beneath the bed again. I couldn't allow fear to come into play. I had to be stronger, not show her that she had gotten under my skin.

I went into the bathroom. I turned on the faucet and splashed water on my face. I had deep, dark circles beneath my eyes. I looked as exhausted as I felt. As exhausted as Megan had seemed today.

I blinked and someone stood directly behind me. Someone I couldn't see...but I felt them. I felt cool air surround me, sending goose bumps along my flesh. There was also a pressure on my back, like whoever it was stood so close, their heavy breathing in my ear.

Invisible hands moved up my sides.

They had my full attention...I was just afraid to let them know it.

Creeped out, I walked into my room. The drawing of Mount Hood was upside down. In fact, every single picture on my wall was upside down.

Overwhelming fear gripped me—a creepy sensation that raced along my spine and wouldn't let go.

I ripped my blanket off the bed, grabbed a pillow, and started for my door. I stepped on something cold. I stopped, lifted my foot, and stuck on the very bottom of it was a razorblade.

Not again...

I picked the blade off my foot and then without another thought ran it across the pad of my thumb, a good inch, watching as the blood beaded and then the crimson stream raced down my arm, dripping onto the floor.

Instantly I felt release, followed shortly by guilt.

What the hell was I doing? Why had I done that? It's like I had no control over my own body.

"You cannot escape me. I am everywhere. There is not a minute you are alone. I am always there."

"I sense you."

"I feel you."

"I am you."

I reached for the doorknob and it slipped from my fingers. A second later, invisible arms encircled me and I was tossed back and thrown onto the bed. Hands grasped either one of my arms and held me captive. Panic welled up inside me. What felt like long hair fell across my face.

Everything within me said to close my eyes and keep them tight, and yet in that moment I saw my friends' faces flash before me, one by one. As easy as it would be to give up—to succumb to the darkness that consumed me—I couldn't allow it. Laria was tormenting everyone I cared about.

"Show yourself, you fucking coward."

The words hadn't left my mouth when I was abruptly lifted up by my ankles, and dangled several feet above my bed. A forceful grip tightened around one ankle, dropping the other. How could a girl, who weighed roughly the same as me, hold me up? Cruel laughter vibrated in my ears and I saw a flash of my mother after the wreck. It was horrible. Even worse than I'd imagined. I had always believed there had been a reason I'd been knocked unconscious during the wreck, so I wouldn't have to see what had happened to her. I realized now how right I'd been. Now, the blinders were off. "Stop it," I cried, but the images burned in my mind, flashing over and over again.

Through the veil of my hair I saw others in the room...the individuals in black robes. Apparently, like Laria and Randall, they weren't happy that I had gone to their hiding place.

"Mom...Anne Marie, please help me," I said under my breath.

An image of myself on the shower floor—my wrists sliced open—flashed in my mind. At a glance, I knew I was dead.

The razor was now on the bed, next to my hand. Inches away. There was already blood on the comforter from where my thumb had bled.

Sweet release. Do it!

Nails bit into the skin of my ankle, and I returned the favor, gripping onto Laria's ankles, digging my nails into them as hard as I could.

She laughed, obviously taking delight in my attempt at hurting her.

The door opened and Miss Akin appeared.

I abruptly fell onto the mattress.

"What on earth!"

I had no idea how much she had seen because I was face down, and a heavy pressure kept my head buried into the pillow.

"Riley?"

Her footsteps rushed forward. I felt Miss Akin try to pull me up, but her efforts were in vain. "Shane!!!!!!"

Her scream reverberated off the walls.

Blackness beckoned, the hand at my neck unrelenting.

Miss Akin was screaming now, and then the weight at my neck was gone. I rolled onto my back and sucked a breath into my lungs.

"Dear God, what was that?" Miss A asked, standing back with a stunned expression.

"Are they gone, Riley?" Shane asked, and I nodded.

"Is *who* gone?" Miss Akin asked, her brows pinched together.

"The ghosts." Shane sat on the edge of the bed and hugged me.

Miss A gasped. "Anne Marie visited me in my dream last night and she warned me that this would happen," she said absently, staring blankly at us. "Now I'm afraid for what is coming."

She wasn't the only one.

Miss Akin made us hot chocolate and when the sun came up we were all still sitting in the kitchen, looking at each other, trying to understand what was happening. I had let Shane talk, and Miss Akin had listened intently, nodding her head from time to time while saying "dear lord," every few minutes.

She wasn't surprised about Laria. After all, she'd had firsthand experience with her at the séance we'd had with Anne Marie, but she seemed more terrified now than she'd been back then, and for good reason. Seeing your boss's daughter dangling over her bed while being held by an invisible force was a bit tough to wrap your brain around.

She had no idea how bad things were going to get.

"Perhaps you should stay home from school today. You need your sleep," Miss A said.

"No, I've missed too much school already." Plus, I didn't want to tell her that school was one of the few places I had the most peace. And I wanted to see how my friends were doing, especially Megan, who had gone quiet on me. I hadn't received a phone call from her since the slumber party.

"You said that Anne Marie warned you this was coming," Shane said, reclining back all the way in the chair. "What did you mean by that?"

"I had a dream, and when I woke, I swear I saw her at the foot of my bed. It was just a second, just a glimmer, but she was there," Miss Akin said, in a way that sounded like she was trying to convince herself. "Truth be told, she has visited me nearly every night since her death. Actually, I find it comforting."

If I ever doubted at all that Anne Marie was working in tandem with us to help beat Laria, I had my answer.

"That's how I knew something was wrong this morning," she said. "I woke out of a dead sleep and heard her voice telling me to check on you." Miss A looked at me. "Does your father have any idea of what's happening?"

"No, and he won't," Shane said, raking his fingers through his hair. "We have to keep this to ourselves. He wouldn't believe it, even if we tried to convince him."

I was still shaken by the pictures that had flashed through my mind of my mom's death, and of my own death. It had been the second time I had seen a vision of myself in the shower with slashed wrists. Were these visions a warning for me to stop cutting, because I could end up killing myself?

"What do we do now?" she asked.

"Destroy her," I said, hoping Laria heard me. The thing I didn't tell Miss Akin was I had no choice. I had to destroy Laria before she had the chance to destroy me.

Chapter Nine

Peter followed me around school like a lost puppy. Although he didn't talk to me, he did intentional things to get my attention, like rolling pencils off desks, tossing books on the floor, and making as much noise as possible. He had gained my classmates' attention, but I refused to look.

If he kept it up, soon everyone in my classes would think I had telekinetic powers.

Every single time something strange happened in first period, Dana would look directly at me.

Even Aaron seemed a little freaked out, not to mention unusually quiet. I tried to focus on what he was thinking, but I was too distracted. I figured his parents had heard from Mr. Monahan and he was told to steer clear of me.

As the day progressed and Peter kept at it, I began to wonder again if maybe I was wrong. What if Laria had only said the stuff about Peter so I wouldn't have a confidant who was another spirit?

I thought back on that day in the library when I'd looked up spiritual possession on the Internet. Peter hadn't left my side, and he hadn't tried to deter me from searching, either. In fact, when I asked him what he knew about the subject, he'd answered my questions pretty truthfully...not at all like an evil spirit who had been found out or wanted to derail me.

I was so confused and so tired. I was distracted after only getting a few hours sleep and waking up to Laria. My head hurt, and my exhaustion was catching up with me. At lunch, Kade asked me if I was feeling all right. I'd lied and smiled, telling him I was fine. Cait apologized at least a dozen times about talking me into going to the hill. I told her she hadn't made me do anything, which seemed to pacify her.

Peter followed me home, and he stayed about fifteen steps behind me. I walked over the bridge, glancing at the river but not really seeing it. When Peter was within arm's reach, I stopped in my tracks, ignoring the old lady who watched me from where she sat in her car in front of the market.

I abruptly turned. "Leave me alone."

His eyes widened and he glanced over his shoulder, almost like he expected to find me talking to someone else. "I...what? Riley, what is happening to you? I don't understand what I did to make you so mad."

"Quit masquerading as other people and spirits, especially an innocent little boy."

"What do you mean?" he asked, sounding close to tears. Suddenly it seemed to dawn on him and his eyes widened. "Oh my God... you believe she's me, or that I'm her?"

He sounded so convincing...

I wanted to believe him. Truth be told, I missed the little shit.

With my mind racing, I picked up my pace, broke into a run, and didn't stop until I was home.

I had an hour before I had to be back to school and at the football game. I washed my face, reapplied my makeup, and changed into a sweater. Miss A had mentioned that the nights would start getting cold fast, and she wasn't kidding. The wind would pick up and the temperature dropped *really* fast.

The football game had already started when I got there. I texted Cait and she immediately texted me back and said she'd come down to meet me. I was grateful. I hated walking into any social event alone.

One nice thing about the after school games is that they weren't as well attended as the Friday night or Saturday afternoon games. And right now, the less people I was around, the better.

Cass walked around the corner and smiled at me. "I didn't think you were going to make it. I've been texting you for the past thirty minutes but you didn't pick up."

I frowned. "You didn't text me until I just now texted you."

She removed her cell from her pocket and showed me the last three text messages, which were all to my phone number.

First Kade and now Cass.

I showed her my recent calls. Zero messages, which was odd come to think of it.

"That's insane," Cass said, and tried to text me again.

My phone signaled I had a text and she frowned.

"Didn't get it, huh?"

"I swear."

She cracked a smile. "I believe you. Come on, we'd better get to the stands. We're at the very top bleacher so we can talk, you know?"

"Good idea."

"Oh, and Kade has been searching for you since the game started."

I grinned, anxious to see him too.

We walked up the bleachers, and I ignored Dana and her friends who were sitting right in the middle of the small crowd. I just kept walking right past them.

I was stunned to see Milo and Richie sitting beside Megan. They normally never made sports events, but Milo was even more attentive to Megan. He obviously realized how serious Laria was. The problem was, anyone associated with me had a reason to be scared. Look at Anne Marie—I still believed her death was connected to Laria. Maybe there was such a thing as being scared to death...

We took a seat in the bleachers, and Richie planted himself right next to me. "I hear you have a ghost haunting you."

"As a matter of fact, I do," I said, glancing at his hand that was resting right against my hip.

I liked Richie, but I think he enjoyed making me uncomfortable. Maybe it was because I knew Kade didn't exactly appreciate the way Richie flirted with me.

"If you ever need anyone to spend the night with you," he scooted a little closer, "you know, to protect you. I'm your man."

I smiled and shook my head, grateful for the lighthearted comment. If any of my friends, guys included, spent one night in my house and saw what I saw, I wondered just how cocky they would be by morning.

I saw Cait making her way up the bleachers toward us. Mrs. MacKinnon and Maddy took a seat beside another mother and her young kid. Maddy didn't look too thrilled to be stuck sitting with her aunt, and gave us a yearning glance.

Milo leaned in. "So, Ri...you're psychic. Does that mean you can read my mind?"

Megan hit him in the arm and scowled. "Quit being a dick."

He rubbed his bicep and laughed. "What, babe? I'm curious. It's intriguing...I've never known anyone who was psychic before."

Cait planted herself right in front of me, and I was forced to move my feet from where I'd had them on the bench.

"Shane has the ball," Cait said, leaning back against my knees.

I smiled, proud of him and wished our dad could pull himself away from his girlfriend long enough to come watch him play before the season was over. The crowd groaned when Shane missed a goal by inches.

"Bloody hell, he just about had it," Milo said, sounding surprised.

Within a few minutes Shane had another chance. Kade kicked the ball to him, and Shane nailed the shot.

Milo and Richie were on their feet before anyone else, and Cait squeezed my hand. Megan glanced at us, and I saw a flash of jealousy in her eyes. I wasn't sure if it was our friendship that made her jealous or if it was the fact Cait liked Shane and vice versa.

When the visiting team took possession of the ball, Cait glanced at Cass. "So tell me, have you been car shopping with your dad yet?"

She shook her head. "No, not yet...but on Sunday he promised we'd visit his friend in Edinburgh, a broker who deals in luxury vehicles."

"Luxury vehicles," Cait repeated haughtily.

Cass rolled her eyes. "I didn't mean it like that." She lifted her chin and grinned. "But it does mean that Daddy is listening."

"Anytime you want to switch rigs, we can do that." Milo gave her a wink.

"Uh, that would be a cold day in hell."

"I like Milo's van," Megan said defensively.

Cass's lips quirked. "Yeah, we know you do. It's the only place you can shag without being bothered."

Megan's cheeks turned bright red.

As they continued to give each other shit, from the corner of my eye I saw movement on the bleachers to the left of me. I glanced and about ten feet away sat Peter. He faced us, knees to chest, arms wrapped around his legs. I straightened and sat back a little, hiding behind Richie.

Maddy kept looking at us over her shoulder. Cait motioned for her to come sit with us. Maddy said something to Karen, who glanced our way and nodded. Maddy immediately started up the bleachers toward us.

Maddy smiled seeing me, but looked hesitant when she looked at Milo and Richie. I understood her hesitation. I didn't know many twelve-year-old girls who wouldn't be a little intimidated sitting with seventeen-year-old boys.

She took a seat beside Cait on the bleacher in front of me. "Hey you." I gave her a quick hug and her gaze immediately shifted to where Peter was sitting.

Peter moved closer, and I returned my attention to the game. Kade was talking with the coach, hands on narrow hips. He was nodding at what the coach was saying, but I could see his gaze scanning the crowd.

I was stunned when across the field I saw a flash of black move behind the visitor dugout. *And it begins*, I thought to myself.

The minutes ticked by and sweat broke out on my forehead. I tried to focus on the conversation around me, but it was impossible with the familiar figures that were filing into the bleachers and standing at the very bottom, looking up at us. One spirit in the middle lifted their hands to the cowl and pulled it back off their head. Laria...and she was looking right at me.

"No," Maddy said under her breath. She was looking at Laria.

This was one time I wished no one else could see what I was seeing.

"What's wrong?" Cait asked. She glanced at me, but I didn't drop my gaze from Laria's. In my peripheral vision I still could see Peter.

Oh my God...

Randall appeared behind Laria and flicked open a pocketknife. My pulse skittered. Had they somehow gotten a hold of Cait's knife yesterday?

Laria started moving forward, her feet not touching the ground, speeding faster up the bleachers straight for me.

"This isn't happening," Maddy said under her breath, and squeezed her eyes closed.

"*Riley, watch out!*" Peter yelled, warning me.

"What are you guys seeing?" Cait asked, looking as terrified as I felt.

Laria kept coming, so fast, Randall right behind her. I couldn't move out of the way fast enough. Maddy put her hands over her head, and everyone with us was terrified.

A second later, I felt the rush of energy spike through me, my heart quickening, my stomach tightening, my head snapping back fast. My head would have hit the bar behind me if it hadn't have been for Richie snatching me back.

"What the hell was that?" Richie said, his arm around my shoulders. "You could have gone right over the back of the bleachers."

Milo jumped up. "I felt like a rush go through me. Did you all feel it?"

No one said anything, except Maddy who nodded.

I couldn't catch my breath. I'd never had a panic attack, but I'm pretty sure I was having one now.

Riley, are you all right? Peter asked.

"Yes," I said, feeling terrible that I'd let Laria convince me he wasn't real.

I was on the verge of tears, my thoughts scattered, my emotions all over the place.

"I'm sorry, Peter. She told me that she was you." The words were out before I could stop them.

Richie frowned. "Um, who are you talking to, Ri?"

"A dead little boy is who she's talking to," Maddy replied, appearing almost irritated by the question.

"How do you know?" Milo asked, and everyone in our group turned to look at her.

Cait stood. "I think we should take Riley for a walk or something. It's not safe for her to be sitting up here any longer."

I didn't feel at all well. In fact, I felt so nauseous, I wasn't sure I would make it out of the bleachers before I lost my lunch. Thankfully I did, though. My friends were on my heels.

"Maddy, go with Mum," Cait said. It was the first time I had heard her refer to Karen as *their* mum.

Not surprisingly, Milo lit up a blunt the second we were inside his van.

He inhaled so deeply that his eyes rolled back in his head before he handed it off to Richie.

"We're in the school parking lot," Cait said, stating the obvious.

"I can't wait," he said, his voice squeaky as he exhaled and blew a stream of pot smoke over our heads. "I'm freaking out."

"Great, now we're all going to be high," Megan said, and reached for the door. All the girls followed her out.

"You don't want to get high?" Megan asked Cass, looking surprised.

"No, I need to lay off that shit for a while," she said, giving me a sideways glance as I leaned against the lamppost. "I end up eating too much junk food anyway, and my pants are already tight as it is."

As the minutes ticked by, the nausea I'd been experiencing began to wane and I felt guilty for leaving the game, especially when Kade had wanted me there, and Shane was having such a good game.

I could stay and chance another go-around with Laria, or I could go home and try to find more ways to protect myself, because what I was doing wasn't enough. Plus, I felt like I was slowly coming unwound, and I didn't want to fall apart in front of an audience that included Dana and her friends.

It was bad enough that rumors were circulating in school about me throwing myself down the stairs, cutting, and Kade's infidelity. I didn't need people saying I was losing my mind on top of it. I'd already seen Richie's expression when I'd been talking to Peter. Even though he knew I was being haunted, and I was psychic, he still looked a little terrified of me.

"I'm gonna go," I said, and started walking.

"No." Cait grabbed my arm. "You can't go alone. I'll walk with you."

"We can drive you," Megan said, heading back for the van.

Honestly, my head was starting to pound, and I didn't feel like inhaling pot smoke. "Can you take me?"

Megan nodded. "Sure." She cracked the van door open and Milo appeared.

"I'm taking Riley home."

"I'll go with you," he said, his tone making it clear he wasn't going to take no for an answer.

"But my car isn't that big."

He pointed to his van.

"No, we'll take my car," Megan said.

Everyone walked toward the car. Apparently they felt there was safety in numbers, because no one stayed behind. I didn't blame them for being freaked out. I didn't like that they were being pulled into something they had no control over.

I actually felt bad for Maddy since she was the only other one to actually see the spirits. Like me, she would never forget what she had seen tonight.

A burning sensation started at the base of my neck and followed down my spine to the waistband of my jeans. I winced and sucked in a breath.

"You okay?" Megan asked, putting a hand on my shoulder.

I nodded.

"You're lying," Milo said. "I can see fear in your eyes. You're fuckin' scared and it's all right to say it."

Megan shifted on her feet. "Maybe I should stay the night with you. I mean I'm sure my mom would let me. Considering the circumstances, it makes sense. Maybe then I won't have such horrible dreams."

Milo's back straightened. No doubt the thought of his girlfriend staying in his buddy's house was a bit disconcerting. Cait dropped her gaze to the ground between us. She obviously didn't want Megan staying at my house either.

"I would think the dreams would be worse, especially since this chick has been haunting Riley since she moved here," Milo said, chewing his lip ring.

"I'm all right," I blurted, keeping the burning pain that was searing down my back to myself. "Thanks, though. I appreciate it." I became lightheaded and a pain exploded in the back of my head. I was so tired, and the weight of my limbs felt overwhelmingly heavy, as if I had to walk more than a few steps I would go down.

Megan grabbed my hand. "I'm taking you home right now."

I sat in the passenger's side of Megan's car while Cass, Cait, Richie, and Milo piled in the back. Thank God I lived close.

Megan hit the speed bump faster than she should have, and the car scraped from the weight in the backseat.

Cass snorted. "Didn't I say I was eating too much shit lately?"

I smiled, grateful for the humor.

"Are you sure you don't want me to stay with you?" Megan offered again, looking concerned.

Before I had time to respond, another wave of dizziness washed over me, and this time I had to rest my head against my knees.

"This is bad." Cait sounded as frustrated as I felt.

Within a minute we were in front of the inn. I opened the car door and immediately my gaze was drawn to the upstairs window, and the room that was directly across the hall from mine.

A tall figure with thin stringy hair stared back at me.

Randall.

I steadied my nerves, wishing my dad was home.

Cait followed my gaze, and must have seen by my expression that someone was there watching us. "Screw this. You are not going in there alone."

I couldn't talk my friends out of coming with me.

We filed up the steps to my room, and Miss A was on our heels. I started to sweat, and quickly ditched my sweater.

Richie glanced at Milo and smiled.

I had a tight cami on, but you'd think by Richie's expression that I was wearing just my bra.

I was more exhausted than I'd ever been. I sat on the edge of my bed, and glanced up at Miss Akin, who stood in the doorway. "What is wrong, my love?" she asked.

"I feel sick," I said, taking a few deep breaths, hoping the wave of nausea that hit me would pass.

A high-pitched noise sounded in my right ear.

Miss Akin turned to my friends. "Did she take something I should know about?"

Cait shook her head. "Nothing. We swear, Miss A."

"Yeah, we promise," Megan replied, and Cass nodded.

"I didn't take anything, Miss A," I said, curling up on my bed in the fetal position. "I just need to sleep."

"Where's Shane?"

"The game is still going," Milo said, scratching the back of his neck. "Maybe we should head back."

"Milo, will you bring Shane home immediately after the game?" Miss Akin asked.

"You got it, Miss A."

Miss Akin took a deep breath, then released it with a controlled smile. "You should all go now. Riley needs her rest."

"I'll call you," Cait said, and I nodded. She leaned down, kissed my forehead.

"Feel better, okay?"

I nodded. "I already do."

She didn't believe me. None of them did. I felt their fear. They had a right to be terrified.

Every one of them hugged me goodbye before Miss Akin shooed them out of the room. I heard her ramble on as she walked them out.

Across the hall, the door opened. Someone stood there, in the doorway of the other room. The floor creaked as they stepped closer.

The breath in my lungs froze as I waited for another sound.

Riiiiillllllleeeeyyyy.

I desperately wanted to scream for Miss A, but I was paralyzed with fear. I squeezed my eyes closed. A strange dragging sound followed, and I couldn't bring myself to open my eyes.

Mom, help. Please make it go away.

I immediately envisioned a bubble surrounding me, a protection exercise from one of the books I'd read.

A man's cruel malicious laughter vibrated in my ears as a cool rush of air rose up to greet me.

"You will not fight me on this tonight, my love," Miss Akin said, and I gasped. I was so relieved to see her plump face when I opened my eyes. She had a couple of pill bottles in her hand and she removed a tablet from each. "I poured some apple juice so you can wash them down. I will not have you losing any more sleep. I just cannot have it. I am half tempted to call your father and tell him to come home immediately."

"No," I said, taking the pills from her and downing them in one swallow, chasing it with the juice. If she called Dad, he would have me on lockdown. "He'll be home soon enough as it is. No need to scare him more."

Her face mirrored the concern in her voice. "But he can help you, my dear."

If only that were true...

Chapter Ten

The pills did what they were supposed to do. Within twenty minutes I felt the lull of sleep and I welcomed it, but I forced myself to stay awake until Shane got home and I had a chance to talk to Kade.

Miss Akin sat in the chair, crocheting a sweater for a friend's grandchild, a little pink sweater that spoke of innocence. She smiled at me in her comforting way, but I saw something else there. Fear. I didn't know if she feared for me or actually feared me. I had seen that same look earlier on my friends' faces.

Despite my best effort to stay awake, I nodded off, but I heard Shane's voice.

"What happened?" he asked, the bed shifting beneath his weight as he sat beside me.

"She wasn't feeling well," Miss Akin replied. "I gave her a pill for nausea...and one for pain."

"Did you call Dad?"

"She didn't want me to."

"I can understand," he said, his palm flattening against my forehead.

I cracked my eyes open and smiled.

"Hey you," he said, his lips curving, but I could see the concern on his face. "I'll crash in here tonight, okay?"

I nodded.

The chair creaked as Miss A stood. "I'll keep my door open, just in case you need anything."

He walked her to the door. "Actually, you might lock it."

I wanted to tell him that no lock on earth would keep Laria away. That she was capable of so much more than any of us gave her credit for. If all of them knew the truth, I wondered what they would do.

I had to give Miss A credit for sticking it out with us. I didn't know of many people in her position who would.

I was taken back to another time...

The landscape changed the moment we came over the mountains. The dreary carriage ride went from bumpy and jarring to halfway pleasant as we made our way onto the main road that led to Braemar.

My father glanced up from his book to stare at me, as was his custom. I hated the white wig, preferring instead his usual ginger locks. But he was playing lord of the manor for all it was worth this day.

"You are Laird and Lady MacKinnon's guest, and that means I expect you to behave as a guest would."

He did not fool me for a minute. I knew what he intended. He expected this trip to yield a marriage proposal. Soon I would be eighteen, and on the shelf, so to speak.

I was not opposed to marriage. I knew it was my lot in life—especially being the eldest of five daughters. I just never imagined my family would be in such a hurry to be rid of me.

I was also aware of the rumors circulating throughout our household. I had been told on more than one occasion, from both parents and my siblings, that I was spending far too much time in the company of Thomas, a footman in our home.

The first time I had seen Thomas was when I'd returned from boarding school for the holidays. We'd been attracted to each other—friends and kindred spirits from the moment I saw him sitting on the back stoop, and shooting to his feet the second he saw me, as though he expected to be reprimanded for sitting down. I had smiled and told him to not worry.

Soon we became inseparable, spending his free hours together. I liked him more than a friend, and fancied what our life would be like together. That is until he told me about a young seamstress who worked in a small, nearby village. He had fallen hopelessly in love with her, and they were saving money to one day buy their own parcel of land, to move away, since her father did not approve of Thomas.

I would never reveal his secret. I knew he had been ready to leave when he'd learned I was being sent away for the summer. But I had stopped him, and even lied and told him that I wished to go to Braemar, to see the MacKinnons. I knew they were good friends of the family, and even vaguely recalled the four children, but I had been very young when last we'd met.

In the distance I saw the castle sitting on the small knoll, surrounded by tall fir trees. The castle wasn't nearly as lovely as my own home, but I preferred the idyllic setting to the somewhat barren landscape of my family's manor. The river would be a quick walk and I already anticipated I would be spending many hours there.

Taking a deep, steadying breath, I felt my father's gaze and made eye contact.

His brows instantly furrowed.

I'd always been intimidated by him. A military man, he hated when anyone, particularly a woman, looked him straight in the eye. "For the love of God, Margot, sit up straight."

It seems I could never do anything right.

"Yes, sir," *I replied, doing as he asked while squeezing my gloved fingers together to keep from screaming.*

As the carriage rolled onto the gravel leading onto the castle drive, people stepped out of the castle's doorway. They were all dressed far more casually than my father and I were, and I breathed an inward sigh of relief.

"Now remember, you speak only when spoken to. You are the MacKinnons' guest and you shall act accordingly. Is that understood?"

"Yes, sir."

I smoothed out the skirts of my floral gown—one of several new dresses my parents had given me, no doubt to impress the man that they wished for me to marry.

My dad exited the carriage first and I could hear him share pleasantries with the MacKinnons.

I forced a smile as I stepped from the carriage.

A middle-aged man with dark hair and blue eyes approached. "Miss Murray. We are so very pleased to have you with us. It has been far too long. How lovely you are."

Lady MacKinnon was strikingly beautiful—her skin like porcelain, her dark hair worn up. She had such fine features and amazing eyes—brilliant blue eyes that radiated warmth and kindness. "May I call you Margot?" *she asked, and I nodded, knowing already that we would get on well.*

Two girls ran out, one about my age, the other slightly younger, their smiles welcoming.

"My sons are out hunting now, and you will meet them at dinner."

I opened my mouth to respond, but my father beat me to it. "She is looking forward to meeting them."

"Please, come in," Laird MacKinnon said as two servants rushed past us and picked up my trunk.

Laird MacKinnon lifted a brow at my father. "Will you not be staying, Marcus?"

My father shook his head. "Nay, I must return home immediately... though I do have time for a brandy."

Of course he had time for a brandy. He always had time to drink.

The youngest MacKinnon daughter had given up her room during her visit, telling me that she was happy to share with her sister, and I was grateful for her generosity.

As I settled into my room, I heard my father's booming voice as he talked about himself. What did I expect? After all, he was his own favorite subject.

I watched him leave an hour later. He had not even bothered to say goodbye.

I stood at the window and watched as the carriage took him away, back home. It was strange how much relief I felt at seeing the carriage diminish into a spot on the horizon. I lay my hands against my tightly corseted waist and released the breath I'd been unconsciously holding.

I nearly stepped away from the window when I saw two riders approach. They waved as they passed the carriage, and I watched with anticipation the closer they came. Both men carried bows and arrows, and had some kind of small animal hanging from the saddle. They were young men—both with dark hair, one wearing his tresses longer, rakishly.

I smiled.

Ian and Duncan. The beautiful MacKinnon brothers.

Duncan glanced up at the window and my breath caught in my throat. I knew I should step away, but I didn't. He lifted his hand and waved. Instinctively, I waved back. Following his gaze, Ian looked up at the window.

He didn't wave, but instead gave a curt nod...and flashed a smile that made my heart skip a beat.

I could feel heat race up my neck to my cheeks.

Anticipation rushing through me, I stepped away from the window and went to the wardrobe. Lady MacKinnon had said that supper would be at five o'clock. A servant had already come in and unloaded my things, putting my dresses in a wardrobe.

I nearly wore the same gown I'd arrived in, but it was so crumpled that I changed, wearing a simple, yet stylish, light green dress.

Ian's youngest sister came to get me, and we walked into the dining room.

Ian stood at the fireplace, talking to his brother.

Dressed in charcoal breeches, knee-high black boots and a navy shirt, Ian looked the epitome of the son of the Scottish laird that he was. "Miss Murray, it is a pleasure to make your acquaintance," he said, coming toward me in long strides. He lifted my hand and kissed the tops of my fingers.

A delicious shiver rushed along my spine.

I remembered every story I had ever heard about him. How at the age of fifteen he had seduced the very married twenty-one-year-old Duchess of Lancaster. The woman had taken one look at him and been tongue-tied all night. It was said the two had began a heated love affair. I had doubted the rumors before, but now I could understand how the young duchess could have fallen head over heels in love with the handsome young Scot. His brilliant blue eyes were amazing, in such contrast to the dark, nearly black hair that fell to his collar and curled. His lips curved, flashing a wolfish smile that revealed straight white teeth. He had the kind of face I yearned to stare at and study for hours on end.

And apparently I was staring, because I heard Ian's sisters giggle.

"It is a pleasure, sir," I said after too long a pause.

"Please, let there be no formality between us. Call me Ian."

I nodded. "Very well, Ian."

"And may I call you Margot?"

"You may."

His brother approached and gave a formal bow. He was handsome as well—his hair not quite as dark nor as long as Ian's, and his eyes a forest green.

"Welcome to Braemar Castle."

"Thank you," I replied.

A servant walked in, a lovely girl with long brown hair and mysterious dark eyes. Seeing me, she hesitated, and then forced a smile. When our gazes met, I could see the anger there, and felt hatred coming off her in waves.

"Laria," another servant hissed at the girl, and she blinked and moved quickly, pouring wine into the goblets.

Laria watched me closely, something I was unaccustomed to in my household, where my father made sure the servants used a separate entrance and were to be "invisible" to family and guests. A flogging would be in place for any servant who did otherwise. This servant would have been released from duty immediately.

I tried to remember if I had seen her before when the family had come to visit, but I did not recall her.

The way she watched Ian though made me realize where the anger came from.

She desired Ian.

"Riley."

I woke up. The sheets were tangled around my hips, and it was morning.

Anne Marie sat at the edge of my bed, her form nearly transparent. I could see straight through her.

"Anne Marie," I whispered.

"Hello, my dear."

Tears burned the backs of my eyes.

"Do you remember?" Anne Marie asked. "Do you remember when you were Margot Murray?"

The information hit me like a ton of bricks. *I* had been Margot Murray during Ian's lifetime? No wonder I had felt so drawn to the castle upon coming to Braemar. I'd felt an unmistakable pull that I'd never quite understood. In fact, I'd been drawn to the castle the first day, where I had cut myself on the very grounds...and where Ian had made himself known to me in this lifetime.

Now it made sense why we'd had such chemistry.

My mind raced. And I had known Laria in that life.

I wish I wouldn't have woken up. I wish I could have seen more.

"When you go to sleep at night, ask for the information to come," Anne Marie said with a soft smile. "Ask to see more of that life, to answer questions you may have."

Was it really that simple? I wondered, remembering the connection we'd had back in that life. It was the same feeling I'd had when I had met Kade.

Chapter Eleven

egan sat a bowl of chocolate ice cream in front of her little brother. Only five years old, he looked nothing at all like Megan. He had platinum blond hair and clear blue eyes, and they also had different last names. In fact, he looked like he could be Cass's little brother instead of Megan's.

Her mom had been getting ready for work in the only bathroom in the trailer that sat on the family friend's property. I could tell Megan was embarrassed the second we walked in, grabbing three empty beer bottles off the coffee table, and emptying an overflowing ashtray into the full trashcan. "Jesus, like it would bloody kill her to clean up after herself."

Her brother glanced at her, large blue eyes wide. "You want me to help you clean?"

She ruffled his hair and smiled. "No, you just eat your ice cream."

Immediately, he relaxed, sitting back on the well-worn couch and digging into his ice cream.

She motioned for me to follow her into the dining room, where I took a seat in one of the three chairs at the small table. Megan decided her house would be the best place to discuss the specifics about Saturday's search for Laria's grave. Plus, she had to watch her little brother again while her mom worked.

"I'm glad we have a few minutes before everyone else shows up," she said, taking a seat across from me, glancing toward her brother, who was completely consumed with the cartoon he was watching.

"I'm freaking out a bit, and I had some questions for you. Questions I've been afraid to ask until now."

"You can ask me anything."

"Can she kill me?" she blurted, keeping her voice low enough that her brother couldn't hear.

I swallowed past the knot in my throat. "I don't know."

"That's hardly reassuring."

I wasn't going to lie to her. All my friends had seen what had happened at the football game last night.

Something hit the floor with a bang in another room. "Motherfucker," a woman shouted, and my eyes widened.

Megan closed her eyes and sighed. "She's so embarrassing."

"I can't find a goddamn thing in this house!" her mom shouted. "What bloody time is it, Megan?"

"Quarter 'til, Mum."

This was the first time I was meeting Megan's mom and I was anxious. She hadn't talked about her much.

A petite, overly-tanned woman, with thin bleached hair that fell to the middle of her back, walked out into the dining room wearing skin-tight jeans and a white wife-beater with a black bra underneath. A pair of black motorcycle boots finished off the outfit.

"You're wearing my jeans again," Megan said, sounding disgusted.

I'd always been amused when I saw an older woman trying to

look younger by wearing clothes from the junior department, but I'd never really known that mom personally...until now. Megan had forewarned me about her mom acting like she was young. In her prime, she must have been a total hottie, but time and a hard life had caught up with her.

She grabbed a pack of menthol cigarettes off the kitchen counter, pulled a cigarette out with a French manicured finger and lit it. She breathed the smoke in deeply and released it through her nose.

She didn't exactly scream class.

"Mum, my paycheck paid for those jeans. I'd appreciate it if you'd take them off, especially since you look ready to bust a seam."

"They fit me just fine, thank you very much," she said, barely sliding her fingers into the pocket as she tried to make a point. "And for your information, my paycheck goes toward the roof over your head and the food in your belly, so if I want to wear your damn jeans, I bloody well will."

"I'm seventeen. It's your job to put a roof over my head."

She stuck out her tongue and picked a piece of tobacco off the tip, then flicked it at Megan.

"Sick," Megan said, looking ready to cry.

I wanted to escape out the back door, especially since her mom hadn't bothered to acknowledge me at all. Maybe she'd already decided she didn't like me without meeting me. Unless, Megan had told her about what was going on.

"Seriously, Mum, those jeans are new and I don't want them all stretched out. I don't wear your clothes."

"Fucking hell," Megan's mom said, balancing her cigarette on the edge of the side table, removing her boots by the heel-toe method, and then unbuttoning and unzipping the jeans, before wriggling out of them. Before I could blink she stood in hot pink lace panties.

Throwing the jeans at Megan's head, she left the room with a final "bitch" comment, and stormed off. A large heart with angel wings was tattooed on her lower back and disappeared into her panties. She had a banging body for her age, I'd give her that.

"Kill me," Megan said, rolling the jeans up in a ball and walking toward the laundry room off of the kitchen. She reappeared a second later. "You're so lucky you have Miss A."

I *was* lucky to have Miss Akin, but I'd give anything to have my mom back. I wanted to tell her that, and maybe to add that she should appreciate her mom while she was here, but I didn't want to go there. My mom had never called me a bitch, or wore my clothes, or made me babysit my brother. I get why Megan was exhausted by the relationship and was already excited to attend university. I would be, too.

Megan's mom walked out a few minutes later, wearing a leather vest over the wife-beater, a pair of black pants that didn't fit nearly as tightly, and a pair of four-inch heels. She reached down, picked up the motorcycle boots, and huffed them toward what I assumed was her bedroom.

"By the way, Mum—this is my friend Riley," Megan said. "Ri, this is my mom, Lena."

For the first time since I'd arrived, her mom actually looked at me. She had the same brown eyes as Megan.

"Hello, Riley," she said, her gaze shifting over me, and I had the feeling she was taking in everything at a glance. I didn't want to head -tap, but a part of me couldn't help it. I was curious.

She had been used by men a lot in her life, and I got the feeling she wasn't exactly the kind of girl who had a lot of close girlfriends, either. She was more comfortable in the company of men and took a lot of care in her appearance because she thrived on men's compliments.

"Ice cream before dinner. Really?" Lena glanced at her son, before tossing the lighter into her crochet purse.

"It's a snack, Mum. I probably won't make dinner until after six o'clock tonight. Remember, I told you my friends were dropping by."

"Only for an hour or two. After that, you need to get your home-work finished." Lena glanced at me. "You hear that, Riley?" Her voice was firm, but there was a quirk to her lips.

I nodded.

Someone knocked at the door and then walked in before Lena could answer it.

"Come in, why don't you," Lena said, scowling at Cass.

Cass stopped and gave Lena the once-over. "Uh, the 70s called—and they want their outfit back."

"Bitch," Lena said.

"Sllllluuuuuttt," Cass replied.

My eyes widened, but Lena just laughed and slapped Cass on the butt.

Cait walked in and Lena smiled tightly. "Cait."

"Lena," Cait said, taking a seat to my right.

"I'll be home at three," Lena said, opening the closet door and taking a long sweater off a wire hanger. She said goodbye to her son and was out the door a second later.

"She seems nice," I said.

Megan lifted her brows but said nothing.

Cass was already going through the cupboards. "I'm so freaking hungry."

"I thought you were on a diet." This came from Megan, who smoothed her hair back from her face and released a loud yawn.

Slamming the cupboard doors closed, Cass walked back to the chair and fell into it. "Thanks for reminding me."

Beside me, Cait snickered. "Cass, you're always on a diet."

"Nice," Cass said.

"You look incredible," Cait replied, and she meant it. "And Johan doesn't seem to be complaining."

Cass completely blew off the last comment. She'd been quiet since announcing at Milo's party that Johan wanted to hook up. There didn't seem to be a lot of dating going on, but Cass didn't seem to mind complaining.

"My birthday party is coming up in a couple of weeks and I want to look good."

Megan got us all some tea, and we were talking when Milo walked in. "Ladies," he said.

Cass looked at Megan with a frown. "*Really?* I thought we were going to discuss some things."

Milo slapped a hand over his heart. "Jesus, Cass...it's nice to see you, too."

Cass rolled her eyes. "I didn't mean it like that."

"Whatever," he said with a grin. "I know you love me."

"Milo, you want to play video games in my room?" Megan's little brother asked.

"Let's play, kid." Milo picked him up and tossed him over his shoulder. He glanced at Megan. "Don't be too long. I have to be home by five."

We waited until we heard the television in the bedroom turn on.

"Okay, time to spill about Johan," Cait said the second she heard the door shut.

Cassie frowned. "What do you mean?"

Megan lifted a brow. "I saw you get into his car after school."

"I don't know what you're talking about," Cass said, brushing a curl over her ear.

"We're just giving you shit," Cait said. "Hey, I'm not judging. Just admit that you're shagging."

She pressed her lips together. "Well...we're having fun together, let's just say that. There's no expectation—from either of us."

I didn't want her to get hurt, and I knew how much she liked Johan.

"Anyway, this weekend," Cait said, scooting her chair closer to the table. "What time are we heading up the hill?"

Megan cleared her throat. "I don't know if I can make it."

Cait narrowed her eyes. "Why?"

"I'm scheduled to work at the library and I really need the money."

I didn't doubt that for a second, and given Megan's fear, I wondered if it might not be better if she stayed home. However, apparently Cait didn't feel the same way. She shook her head. "That's lame."

"Just because you're all into it, Cait, doesn't mean that everyone else is."

Cait glanced at Cass. "What about you. Are you bailing, too?"

"I'm free Saturday." Cass put on some lip gloss and pressed her lips together. "Just promise you'll have me back come Sunday morning, in time for car shopping."

"No one's making any promises." Cait sounded so serious that it took the mood down a notch. "I think only people that want to go should go."

"We'd be down to just the two of us then," I said, almost adding the word "again". "Well, and Kade and Shane. If Megan doesn't go, then I seriously doubt Milo will."

Megan didn't say a word.

Cass leaned back in her chair. "I just don't know how safe it is to go searching for this ghost."

"We're searching for her grave so we can bind her spirit to it and finally give us all some much needed peace." Cait sat up straighter and folded her hands together on the table, all business. "We have a good idea where the grave is, so it shouldn't take too long."

"Maybe I'm just not as brave as you are." Megan sounded irritated. "This scares the shit out of me. Maybe I'm afraid of what she will do if we're all out in the middle of the forest where apparently she and her buddies practiced dark magic. And what if we fail and then things really start to escalate? I know I mentioned it before, but I have to think about my brother. He's so little. Is this going to start affecting him?"

I honestly didn't have the answer to that question. I wish I did. I knew one thing—I wasn't going to force any one of my friends to go searching for Laria's grave.

Chapter Twelve

Friday night the storm came in. Thunder and lightning rocked the inn, and I braced myself for the evening ahead. From what I'd read, spirits manifested from energy and a storm would leave a charge in the air.

Great. I could hardly wait. I had hoped that at least one friend could spend the night, but Mrs. MacKinnon was obviously not too sure about having her daughter stay again two weekends in a row, not to mention she was probably on to the fact that Cait liked Shane, which didn't bode well for any future sleepovers with me.

Megan had to work, but I figured it was just as well. I didn't want her going when she was so uncomfortable about it. She had been through enough already.

The football game had been canceled due to the weather, but the coach had called a meeting to run through some video on their past game instead.

I packed items for tomorrow, including the nail and hammer, and I'd looked up a few extra blessings I'd found in a book Megan had brought to school yesterday. I'd typed them word for word and printed them out.

Miss Akin had gone to bed early, saying she was anxious to dig into her latest feel-good mystery series. Waiting to hear from Kade, I organized my drawers, and when I saw my camera, I pulled it out, walked straight to the window and pulled back the drapes. I remembered the last time I'd stood by the window when it was dark and how Laria had been hanging upside down staring back at me.

My heart hammered in triple time as I snapped pictures of the hillside and the castle. The lightning became more intense, and for the next ten minutes I took nearly two hundred pictures.

I focused most of my attention on the castle. When the lightning let up, I closed the drapes and fell into the chair.

I scrolled through the pictures. Many of the images were too dark, but when the lightning had hit just right, the entire frame was filled with light.

There was one particular picture that intrigued me—a bolt of lightning above the sky, directly behind the castle. The lights were on in nearly every single room, and the ground lights were on, as well.

Frame after frame, different colors emerged, and then one photo made my stomach clench. The castle was cast in red, and in the yard there were what looked to be a group of about six people standing by a tree.

The next frame was the same, but in the frame, along with those six people was a body hanging from a tree.

My blood turned to ice.

I had to get a better look. I rummaged through my desk drawer, looking for the camera cord that would hook to my dad's computer and bring up the pictures so I could get a better idea of what I was looking at rather than on the camera's two by three inch viewer.

When I didn't find the cord there, I went to my closet and sifted through the junk boxes that had been put up on the very top wooden shelf. Standing on the tip of my toes on my vanity stool, I went through each, wading through my sixth grade diary and nostalgic memorabilia. I was on the last box and losing hope that I still had it, when I finally found a few different cords. One looked promising. I tried the small end and it slid into the camera. "Yes, we have a winner."

I raced down the steps to my dad's study, making sure to close the blinds on my way past the window. I hated how his computer faced the wall, so your back was to the door. My mom had always had a thing about facing a doorway so she could see who was entering the room. I completely agreed with her wanting to see who was walking in.

I moved the monitor slightly, so I could at least see any movement in the doorway from the corner of my eye. I plugged in the camera and it immediately started downloading pictures.

I watched expectantly as the pictures flashed before me.

When the last photo finally appeared, I went back to the very first one. The photos of the hillside were still pretty dark. I hit the editing button that brightened the page and looked closer.

One by one, I went through the pictures. It wasn't until I came to the pictures of the castle did the entire feel change. The first dozen pictures the sky was lit up, and then the hue of the pictures started changing to a reddish tone and the figures started appearing in the photos.

There was the suggestion of movement from the castle's courtyard toward a tree, where someone was strung up and hanged.

If I wasn't mistaken, I had cut beneath that same tree, or damn close to it.

Bile rose in my throat.

My heart pounded hard against my chest as I brightened the photo and zoomed in on the figures.

Oh my God.

I felt the blood drain from my face. It was still a distance away, but there was no mistaking the long hair of the woman hanging in the tree or the long gown she wore.

My attention turned to the people who had participated in the hanging. All were men. My gaze was drawn to the castle, and specifically to the window where a silhouette of a person stood in the upstairs window.

My mind raced. That room had been where Margot Murray had been staying during her visit.

A creaking sounded behind me and I let out a gasp.

"Hey," Shane said, as he slid his backpack off his shoulder. He was soaked to the skin. "What are you doing?"

I rested a hand against my chest and tried to relax. "I took some pictures during the lightning storm."

He walked over to me, leaned over my shoulder. "How come it's red?"

"I don't know...but that's not the most interesting thing about the picture. Take a closer look. In fact, let me start from the first frame."

Intrigued, he leaned in closer. Frame by frame he watched, and when I got to the frame where the sky turned red, he tensed.

"What do you see?" I asked.

"Are those people?" he asked, pointing to figures appearing in the courtyard. Sure enough, frame-by-frame followed their progress to the tree. They were huddled up together for most of the frames, until the final few pictures where they strung Laria up.

"You're shitting me," he said, leaning in even closer. "Is that someone hanging?"

His eyes went wide. "Oh my God, you actually caught her hanging on film."

"A hanging that happened over two hundred years ago," I said. "I didn't just take this picture by chance. I felt like I *needed* to take pictures of the hillside and the castle during the storm."

"I remember reading an article about the ghosts of Gettysburg soldiers being caught on film," Shane said, obviously intrigued. "It looks like you have something similar happening here." He chewed his bottom lip. "Did you look through all the pictures?"

"I did, but the photos at the castle are the only ones I saw anything in."

He flipped through the pictures a few times. "Would you mind getting me a pop?" he asked.

I didn't want to, but I went anyway, running to the kitchen. I flipped on every single light as I went along.

I grabbed the pop and ran back into the office. He was now sitting in the chair and he looked over his shoulder at me. "You're not going to believe this."

I didn't like the sound of that.

"What?"

He actually shuddered. "I don't know if I should show you."

"What do you mean?" I said, setting the pop beside him.

"Look at the final frame. Picture one ninety-three."

I kneeled down beside the chair and moved the mouse to picture one ninety-three. I sat back on my heels and squinted. The castle was barely in frame. It was taken directly out my window. "What am I supposed to be seeing?"

"There's a reflection. Do you see it?"

At the same time he lifted a finger to show me the outline, I saw it. The hair on my arms stood on end. I was in the photo, holding the camera to my face, my image reflected back at me in the glass. And directly behind me stood someone.

Laria, pale as I'd ever seen her. Her eyes were almost hollowed out, and she looked nearly skeletal. Her hair and clothing were wet and she had a hand on my shoulder.

Had I felt anything while I'd been taking those pictures? How had I not felt her touching me?

I glanced at Shane. "This has got to stop."

He enhanced the picture further, and as he brightened it, we both gasped. Another figure stood in the room. Randall Cummins... along with several dark cloaked figures.

"I'll never sleep tonight," I said, running a trembling hand down my face. That image would haunt me for the rest of my life.

"I'll crash on your floor."

"Thanks, Shane." There wasn't a chance in hell I was going to decline that invitation.

He unplugged the camera and handed it back to me, then saved the images onto a USB drive. We couldn't keep these on Dad's computer; he'd freak out if he saw them.

Actually, there was a part of me that wanted him to know.

Chapter Thirteen

Saturday morning I woke at seven o'clock to rain pounding against my bedroom window.

Great. Just what I wanted to do—trudge miles uphill in the rain.

Apparently the storm hadn't let up. I went to the window and opened the drapes. There was so much fog, I could barely make out the incline of the hill, and forget seeing the castle.

"Oh shit, is it raining?" Shane asked, sitting up on his elbows.

'Oh shit' was right. "Yeah, it's really coming down, and the fog is so thick I can't see past our backyard."

He let out a groan, stretched and stood. He walked to the window, looked out at the torrential rain and glanced at me. "No way we're going out in this fog."

I'm sure my friends would be elated they wouldn't have to go out grave hunting in the crappy weather.

"I'll text my friends. Will you text Milo and Richie?"

"Done," he said, sending the texts off with lightning speed, and a second later he grabbed his pillow and blanket. "Since we're not going, I'm crashing for a few more hours. You all right in here alone?"

"Yeah, thanks for staying with me."

"No problem." He had one foot out the door when he turned with a reassuring smile. "We'll have peace, Riley," he said, sounding more confident than I felt.

I snuggled under my covers, texted my friends and Kade, and waited for them to respond. Within five minutes all had written back. Kade said he'd be coming by this afternoon. I texted him back and told him to bring his laptop. I was anxious to share the pictures I'd taken.

When he showed up at one, he had Cait with him.

Shane downloaded the pictures I'd taken onto Kade's laptop. Cait actually jumped the second she saw the pictures of the hanging. "That's so creepy."

Kade controlled his emotions a little better. He glanced at me, and I clearly saw the concern there. "So is this like residual energy that was feeding off the storm? I read that traumatic events can be imprinted into the surroundings."

"I don't know," I said. "It could be."

"Check this out, though." Shane brought up the final picture, and Kade leaned in closer. At first he didn't see anything. Then he sat up straight, his eyes wide. "What the hell..."

If anyone still had any question that I was haunted, this picture would eliminate that.

Cait leaned closer. "I don't see what you're talking about..."

Shane pointed it out and she put her hand to her mouth. "Oh my God."

Maybe it hadn't been the best idea to show them.

Kade set the laptop aside and reached for me. I sat down beside him and he slid his arm around my shoulders and kissed the top of my head. "We need to make it to the hill. We'll go tomorrow."

"If the fog is bad, we can't go," Shane said. "I mean, let's face it—if we can't see two feet in front of us down on the valley floor, then what would it be like in the hillside forest?"

He had a valid point.

"Are we overlooking something here? I just don't want this affecting you any more than it already has," Kade said, looking at me. "It's not fair."

It meant a lot to me that he cared so much.

Downstairs the front door opened. "Kids!"

"Dad's home," Shane said unnecessarily. He glanced at Kade. "Dude, you'd better put the computer away before he sees it. He's kind of a dick about us having computers in our rooms."

"I wondered why neither you nor Shane had laptops," Cait said, following Shane to the door.

"Let's just say that Dad working in the computer field hasn't exactly been to our benefit. We've never been allowed to have computers in our rooms, and we can only use the family computer in his office. Nothing sucks worse than having your Mom or Dad walk in when you're Googling po—," Shane's gaze shifted to Cait, who watched him with lifted brow, just waiting for him to finish the sentence.

Shane grinned sheepishly.

Kade cracked up and my heart missed a beat at the sound. I loved hearing that laugh, seeing that smile. I just wanted to crawl into bed with him and not wake up until tomorrow.

But that definitely wasn't happening, especially with Dad home.

We walked single file out of my room and down the stairs. Shane stopped short of the last step, and glanced into the parlor.

Dad was home...and he'd brought company.

Cheryl.

My stomach dropped to my toes. What the hell?

Dad's overnight bag was sitting in the entry, and so was a ridiculously expensive-looking suitcase. What was she doing—moving in?

"Hey kids," Dad said, nodding at Kade and Cait. "You remember Cheryl..."

Kade squeezed my hand. "Of course," I managed, and Shane made a grunting noise.

"Hi, I'm Cait." Cait stepped forward and extended her hand. "I'm Riley's friend."

"And my friend, too," Shane said, and Cait blushed.

Dad lifted a brow at that remark.

"Nice to meet you, Cait," Cheryl said with a warm smile.

I nodded to Kade. "This is my boyfriend, Kade."

Kade glanced at me and grinned. I think he liked the boyfriend label. He walked over to Cheryl and shook her hand. "It's a pleasure."

"The pleasure is mine," Cheryl replied. There was a sheen of sweat on her forehead.

"I'll ask Miss Akin to make us an early dinner. Cait and Kade, if you'd like to stay, you're most welcome," Dad said. Surprisingly enough, he actually looked like he wanted them to stay. Maybe he thought we'd play nice that way.

"Thanks," Kade said. "I'll give our parents a call and see if that's okay with them."

The dining room was dimly lit and Miss A had gone out of her way to make the room cozy and inviting.

Dad and Cheryl sat down, and I took the seat furthest away.

Shane gave me a look that said "kill me" and took the seat across from me, forcing Miss Akin to sit to Dad's right once dinner was served. Cait sat to Cheryl's right, and put her napkin on her lap. She stole a sympathetic glance at me, while Kade squeezed my thigh beneath the table.

Cheryl asked a million questions of Cait and Kade. It was very obvious she was nervous. Truth be told, I was more nervous than anyone. It was tough to make eye contact with her. I hadn't really just stared at her. I'd been too pissed in Edinburgh and preoccupied with the dream I'd had about Kade and Dana. Sitting at the dinner table was a bit different.

What I hated more than anything was that Dad had just sprang her on us. It was one thing to keep her in a hotel room in Edinburgh, but to bring her home—that was too much, too soon in my book.

I glanced up at Shane. His jaw was clenched and he stabbed at the spaghetti. For someone who had been pretty accepting of Dad's new girlfriend to begin with, he didn't seem too thrilled to see her now.

Miss Akin was her jovial self, going out of her way to make everyone comfortable. The spaghetti may as well have been sawdust for all I tasted of it. Dad was trying his best to be a comedian. I actually had forgotten how funny he could be. Kade and Cait genuinely laughed at what he said. I hadn't seen this side of my dad for so long, it kind of surprised me.

Cheryl ate the salad and took a few bites of spaghetti before setting her fork down. She wiped her lips and looked up at me. "I am glad you are recovered from your fall, Riley. What a terrifying experience. Your father has been so concerned about you."

My throat tightened. How much had Dad told her? I wondered. I waited for her gaze to shift to my arms...but she held eye contact.

Then again, why would he tell his new girlfriend that his almost seventeen-year-old daughter was a cutter? No doubt Cheryl's perfect boarding school raised son would never do something so rash and horrifying as harm himself.

"Thanks for your concern." I reached for the bread and nearly knocked my milk over.

Kade steadied the glass and gave me a reassuring smile.

I felt Dad's gaze boring into me.

"Tomorrow Cheryl and I are going to Loch Ness. I thought maybe you kids would like to come along. We're even taking a boat ride...rain or shine." His gaze jumped between me and Shane. "Cait and Kade, you're welcome to come as well."

"Sorry, I have homework," Shane said, taking another bite and chewing slowly.

Dad's gaze shifted to me.

"Yeah, I have homework, too."

Cheryl actually looked disappointed. She sat up a bit straighter and pressed the napkin to her lips. "Miss Akin, would you like to come with us?"

Miss A nodded. "Indeed, I would like very much to go. It's been years since I've visited the loch."

If the weather was crappy again tomorrow, then there was no way we'd be able to head up the hill...but I had no desire to take a boat ride around Loch Ness with my dad and Cheryl in the rain and fog.

Dad proceeded to tell a story about when Shane was six and I was seven, when we'd gotten on the wrong city bus as my mom's back was turned. "For some reason, they were under the impression she was going to meet up with them at home."

"That's what happens when you have a couple of blonde-haired kids," Shane said flippantly.

Cait laughed. "Didn't you think it was strange when your mom wasn't with you?"

Shane shook his head. "I was too busy with my Game Boy, and Riley had discovered her iPod, so she wasn't paying attention either."

"Their poor mother was beside herself," Dad said. "She ran ten blocks after that bus. Damn near caught up with it, too." His smile faded and he looked down at his plate. "Those were good years."

Maybe he missed Mom more than we knew.

"She was an incredible mom," I said. Shane met my gaze and smiled.

"She sounds like quite a woman." There wasn't a tinge of jealousy in Cheryl's eyes. "I know what it's like to lose someone you love. My husband died of cancer a couple of years ago. He was a good dad, and I like to think that he's watching me. That he's with our son, and that he realizes we're doing our best without him."

Dad reached out and squeezed Cheryl's hand. She smiled at him. I saw so much pass between them in that stare, and felt the comfort Cheryl had given him. There was no denying they had both suffered tragic losses.

As silence fell over the table, Dad pushed back his chair. "Well, that was wonderful, Miss Akin. Thank you."

Shane met my gaze, lips quirked. Dad was definitely on his best behavior tonight. Normally he left the dinner table without saying much of anything. Miss A seemed pleased with the compliment, though, as she stood and started clearing the table.

Dad and Cheryl followed us into the parlor and sat down on the loveseat.

Kade and I sat on the couch beside Shane and Cait.

Kade slid an arm around my shoulders. He must have sensed my uneasiness because his thumb brushed along the back of my neck.

"What are we watching?" Dad asked, remote in hand, browsing the channels. He ended up on a documentary about Stonehenge.

Shane glanced at Cait and they laughed under their breath, and promptly excused themselves.

"So, Kade, I understand you're on the football team with Shane," Cheryl said, hands folded in front of her. Dad put a hand on her thigh and I had to look away. It would take some time to get used to seeing him with a woman other than my mom. And intimate touches and kisses were just too much to stomach.

Kade nodded. "I am. We're doing very well this year. Undefeated so far."

Even Dad seemed surprised by that bit of news.

"I'll have to make the next game," he said absently, settling back against the loveseat.

Shane passed by, headed toward the door with Cait in tow.

"Where are you going?" Dad asked.

Shane stopped in mid-step. "Milo's here to pick us up."

Dad checked his watch. "It's seven-twenty."

"We'll be back by nine." Shane glanced at Kade, who seemed surprised his sister was leaving with him.

"I'll be back by nine," Cait said reassuringly.

Kade opened his mouth to say something, but closed it a second later.

I looked at him and smiled. "It's okay. They'll be back."

The door closed and silence fell over the room.

Miss Akin checked in with us a few times, but ultimately said goodnight and went to her room.

I watched the show...but I wasn't really seeing it. Instead, in the reflection of the screen I saw a glow, and what appeared to be a blemish on the screen. The blemish grew larger, until it was the size of a softball, moving a foot back and forth on the screen.

"Do you see that?" I whispered in Kade's ear.

"What is it?"

"It's behind me." I glanced over my shoulder but there was nothing behind us. Not a lamp on a table or anything that would cause a reflection on the screen.

In my right ear, I heard a loud pop, followed by a high-pitched sound.

Behind me I felt movement. Someone stood directly in back of me. On the television's reflection I made out a silhouette of someone. They were dressed in a black robe with a cowl.

Then there was another figure, dressed the same, and then another. One by one, as the seconds ticked by, until the room filled up. I couldn't even make out the furniture in the room behind me. And then Laria stepped forward, cowl down about her shoulders, face pale, malicious smile on her lips. She was behind us, and I saw her reach out and touch Kade, her fingers grazing the top of his head and moving slowly down, onto his shoulder.

I waited for him to react, but he didn't move.

Did he not feel her? Could he not see her in the television's reflection?

Was I just imagining things?

The ringing grew louder and higher.

The picture brightened up on the screen and I couldn't see the reflection. From the corner of my eye I saw Laria's hand, sliding down over Kade's chest.

Laughter sounded in my ear.

I was ready to lose it, to stand up and scream, when Anne Marie stood in front of the television set. She put a finger to her lips. Mentally I could hear her tell me to calm down. "She wants you to react. Don't let her see that she's affecting you."

It was impossible to pretend like Laria didn't exist. How could anyone expect me to ignore what was happening to me? They had to experience it firsthand to fully appreciate the pure terror involved.

Kade glanced at me, his eyes were dark—the slate color I was becoming far too familiar with of late.

He felt cool to the touch.

Leaning his head against mine, he breathed in my ear, "I am everywhere. There is nowhere I can't go, nowhere you can escape to, because I will find you."

Chapter Fourteen

"Miss Murray, do you wish me to tie the stays for you?"

Laria stood at the door to my room, a freshly pressed dress in her hands that she quickly hung up in the wardrobe. "I'd be happy to assist you."

I had just awoken. Ian had asked me to take a walk in the village today. I yearned to be with him. The days had passed far too quickly, and it was as though I expected my father to arrive and announce that he, or my mother, needed me home. I could think of nothing worse than leaving Braemar.

"Yes, thank you," I said, glancing at Laria. Her eyes were such a dark brown, it was difficult to make out the pupils. I smiled and presented my back to her. Something aside from those nearly black eyes made me nervous.

I felt her watch me closely, and had watched Ian's reaction around her. I was not so naive to believe that servants and their employers did not share beds. I knew the whisperings in my own household, but I found it difficult to accept that there was more going on between Ian and Laria than a mutual friendship or perhaps a touch of flirtation, at least by what I had seen pass between them.

"You are up early today," Laria said, pulling hard at the strings. I barely had time to draw breath before my ribs were crushed beneath the corset's stays.

"Aye, I am." I did not feel the need to explain myself. An awkward silence followed, and the moment I slid into the pale yellow day dress, I turned to her. "Thank you for your assistance."

She nodded curtly, and left the room.

I met Ian in the courtyard, and as I walked beside him down the long drive, the sensation of being watched was so strong that I could not resist the urge to glance over my shoulder. I saw Laria standing in my room. She abruptly stepped away from the window, but not before I saw her.

"Come, Margot," Ian said, and I fell into step beside him.

"You are so pensive today," Ian said, tilting his head slightly as he watched me closely.

"Sorry, I was just thinking."

"About?" he asked inquisitively, and then laughed, the sound making me smile. To be around him every single day of my life—that is what I wished for. We got on well together, and I could only hope he felt the same way. Though at the time I hadn't liked my family's decision to send me to Braemar, I was now grateful they had.

"About how happy I am here," I said, before I could stop myself.

He reached out and smoothed a curl over my ear. The touch sent a jolt of pleasure up my spine.

"I am so glad you are happy here, Margot." His thumb brushed along my jaw, before he dropped his hand back to his side.

My heart pounded so loud in my chest, I wondered if he could hear it.

"May I ask...do you miss your home?"

"No," I was quick to answer.

"Surely you miss your family and friends." There was an inquisitive tone to his words.

Had my father told his father about Thomas? I wondered. They were good friends, so perhaps he had been honest, and in my father's mind, he believed I was hopelessly in love with the footman.

Suddenly it was very important that Ian know the truth.

"My father thinks I am in love with a servant," I blurted.

Ian didn't miss a beat. He glanced at me, stepped over a puddle and surprised me by lifting me by the waist, up and over the puddle. His hands lingered on my hips. "And are you in love with a servant?"

"No, of course not. Thomas is my friend."

His lips quirked. "A very lucky friend, indeed." He dropped his hands and began walking.

I followed behind him, wishing he would ask more questions, but he said nothing. I had to assume that someone had mentioned Thomas to him. I hated how people could judge so easily, so harshly, without realizing the truth. No doubt, since I had been whisked away from my home so quickly, people would gossip and believe the absolute worst.

"Ian, I fear you do not understand."

"You owe me no explanation." His strides were so long, I had to run to keep up with him.

I reached out, grabbed his shirt.

He glanced at me, and then the shirt. He arched a dark brow.

I dropped my hand. "I apologize, I did not mean…I just wanted you to know…the truth."

His eyes were suddenly so intense, and I saw a nerve twitch in his jaw. "And what is the truth, Margot?"

I licked lips that had suddenly gone dry. "Thomas is in love with another, and he has planned a life with that person."

"*Do you wish that person were you?*" *he asked matter-of-factly.*

"*When first we met, when I was a girl, I thought him very handsome,*" *I said truthfully.* "*Indeed, I thought we would be a good match, but then he shared his feelings about another. All it took was seeing them together one time and I knew that we would only ever be friends. And, whether you choose to believe it or not, close friends is all we have ever been and will ever be.*"

He stared at me for a long moment. "*You were in love with him?*"

"*I love him, but I am not in love with him...if that is what you are asking.*"

His lips quirked.

I was tired with this game. It was enough that my own family did not believe me, but I had honestly thought Ian was different. I expected him to believe me.

Foolish, foolish girl, I thought to myself.

Frustrated, I turned on my heel and started walking toward the castle.

"*Margot, come back.*"

I didn't stop. I was so angry, the blood in my veins boiled. Here I had bared my soul and he still questioned me. How dare he? I did not interrogate him on his past or his escapades with the Duchess of Lancaster, or God knew how many other conquests.

I heard footsteps behind me, and then felt a hand at my wrist. He pulled me toward him, and before I could speak, I was in his arms and he was staring down at me with those beautiful blue eyes and a smile that melted my heart. "*I did not intend to make you angry. I only wanted the truth.*"

I dropped my gaze to his chest, and I could see a wide slice of skin where his shirt opened at the throat. The pulse fluttered there and I ached to press my lips against that olive skin, to taste it.

"Margot," he said, lifting my chin with gentle fingers. "Thank you for telling me the truth. I wanted—nay, I needed—to know," he said, entwining the fingers of his free hand with mine.

He lowered his head and kissed me.

I had never before been kissed and I liked it.

Actually, I more than liked it.

"I am glad you came to Braemar," he whispered.

My pulse skittered.

He leaned in again, and this time the kiss was deeper, a sweep of his tongue across my lips, asking for entry. I opened to him, and I was not disappointed. Never could I have imagined that this is how it could be. True, I knew there would be passion, but I had not expected this deep ache that welled within me.

When we returned to the house, my cheeks were flushed. I had never been so happy. Ian's kiss had ignited something inside me—something I wished to further explore.

That night before dinner, I had tea brought to my room. It was Laria who served it. Those dark eyes followed me around the room as she poured.

"Do you wish me to help you change, Miss Murray?"

Unease worked its way up my spine. "No, thank you."

Her brow furrowed, but she nodded and left me.

I drank the tea, and by the time the dinner hour came around, I was nauseous.

A knock sounded at my door.

"Come in," I called.

It was Ian's youngest sister. Seeing me lying down in my shift, she frowned. "Dinner is in quarter of an hour."

"I fear I do not feel at all well."

She placed a hand on my forehead. "You do not feel fevered."

"Please tell your mother I am unable to make it to dinner this even-

ing, and how very sorry I am."

"Should I summon a doctor?"

I shook my head. "Nay, I am sure tomorrow I will be fine. It could have been something I ate."

I closed my eyes and when I woke, I found Ian sitting in a rocking chair beside the bed. He had fallen asleep with his elbow on the arm of the chair, chin propped on hand. His dark hair fell across his forehead, and long eyelashes cast shadows against high cheekbones.

My stomach clenched. I could not get over how beautiful he was. How every time I looked at him, my heart would race, and when he kissed me—oh dear God, when he kissed me, I went weak at the knees and felt a flush race through my body, making me come to life.

I had read enough books to know what happened between a man and a woman. I was well aware that a woman was expected to be chaste when she exchanged her marriage vows...but I could honestly say that I understood why some could not resist temptation.

Ian MacKinnon most certainly was a temptation.

He must have felt my stare because he opened his eyes and smiled. "You're awake," he said, and surprised me when he stood and sat on the edge of the bed, his weight making the mattress shift beneath me. "I was alarmed when you did not come down to dinner last night."

I sat up abruptly. "Last night?"

"Indeed, you have been asleep ever since."

He lay down beside me, going up on an elbow.

My eyes widened.

His laughter was at once teasing and mischievous. "No one will come in." He flashed a wolfish smile. "Mother and the girls are in town, and my father and Duncan are at the river, hoping to catch tonight's meal."

"What if a servant comes in?"

"They would not enter without knocking first. Plus, I can always slip *beneath the bed if need be."*

"You're dangerous," I said before I could stop myself.

He cocked his head. "Dangerous...how so?"

He made my thoughts turn positively wicked, and that scared me.

His thumb brushed along my lower lip. "I am glad you are feeling better." He leaned in and kissed me softly on the forehead, the nose, and then my lips.

Chapter Fifteen

The bowling alley was twenty minutes away from Braemar and smelled like old, musty shoes. The entire place was antiquated, looking like something out of a movie set from the nineteen fifties. Since it was a rainy Sunday afternoon, there were quite a few of us there. The owner had made sure to give us two lanes in the center of the alley, no doubt so he could keep an eye on us.

The girls bowled in one lane and the boys in the other.

It was pretty obvious from the second Cass threw her first strike, that she was the one to beat. By the third frame, she had her third strike. She lifted her arms triumphantly and looked directly at Johan, who grinned at her.

Shane also surprised me. I didn't really recall him being that great at bowling when we were younger. He had an impressive technique and threw the ball as hard as he could. I noticed how Cait's eyes were glued to his backside from the second he stepped up to grab the bowling ball to the time he released and turned back to face all of us.

Megan had let go of her jealousy about Shane and Cait, which was a huge relief. She and Milo were meant to be and I would have hated to see anything come between them, or ruin the friendship Shane had with Milo.

Milo was a little too stoned, throwing gutter ball after gutter ball. He just laughed it off.

Like me, Kade was in the middle of the pack. I was glad to see he wasn't too competitive, though I couldn't say the same thing about Cait. It was obvious she wanted to win.

The time away with friends was a godsend and made me forget, at least for a little while, about Laria.

"Riley, your turn," Megan said.

After managing my first spare, I went to sit by Kade, but he pulled me onto his lap. I slid my arms around his neck and relaxed. When I was with him I felt like I could breathe.

Cait watched us with a smile.

Shane sat beside her, his hand moving to her thigh.

She glanced at him and leaned in for a kiss.

Johan yelled triumphantly as he hit a strike, fist-pumping the air.

"Nice," Milo said, high-fiving him.

Cass walked up beside him, and took her ball from the return rack. She waited for him to take his second turn, and I could tell she watched him from the corner of her eye. Tom sat to my left, and I could feel his frustration. He liked her a lot, but she liked Johan... who sort of liked her.

It was Kade's turn after Johan.

Tom immediately approached me and sat down. "Riley, I wanted to apologize for being such a dick to you when you first came to Braemar. You didn't do anything to me and I treated you like shit."

I hadn't expected an apology and yet I appreciated it. "That's okay."

"No, it's really not. You didn't deserve it; I think you're a good person, and Kade is really into you. If you're all right with him, then you're all right in my book."

"Thanks, Tom."

"I also respect you for staying in the mausoleum. I mean, I hope that didn't like...mess you up or anything."

I wasn't quite sure what he meant by that, or if he worried that I'd started cutting after that incident. "If anything, I guess it made me face a fear."

"You've got more guts than any girl I know, I'll give you that," he said, laughing. When he smiled that way he was actually kind of cute.

I glanced at Kade, who had just picked up a spare. He seemed happy I was talking to Tom, and I wondered if he had put him up to it.

"Friends?" Tom asked, putting out a hand.

"Friends," I replied, and shook it.

When I looked up, Cass was giving me the stink eye. She'd fooled around with Tom at a party not so long ago, and the two barely even spoke now. I wasn't going to get all tied up in their drama. I had enough of my own.

At the end of the first game, Megan asked if I wanted to use the restroom, so I went with her. The door was at the end of a long hall, where a mop and pail sat.

The bathroom smelled like pine cleaner and had horrible lighting.

I went to the first stall and closed the door. At least it wasn't dirty.

Megan cleared her throat. "So...Cait and Shane seem happy."

"They are. I think they're good together."

"Yeah, they are."

I was glad she thought so, too.

Megan began brushing out her hair. I could see her through the crack of the door, and she started laughing as she mentioned Cass's love triangle with Tom and Johan.

The door opened and she fell silent.

I zipped up my pants and blew my nose. My gaze abruptly shifted to the floor. Two booted feet stood directly in front of the door of my stall.

Fear rippled along my spine.

They were male boots.

Familiar boots.

I felt the blood drain from my face, and my heart pounded hard against my breast bone.

"Megan," I said, and dared to look through the crack of the door.

Huge mistake.

Randall stared back at me. I screamed...but it was too late.

Oh my God...I was trapped.

He thrust something through the crack. I yelped, and immediately recognized it as the sickle he'd had in my classroom that first day he had shown himself to me.

The door handle jiggled, and then he became more aggressive.

I was so screwed. Although the bowling alley wasn't huge, the high tempo music was cranked, and there's no way anyone would hear us, especially since the bathroom was at the other end of the bowling alley.

The sickle turned abruptly and just barely missed my upper arm.

I stepped back against the wall, and put my leg up to keep the door shut.

"Just give into it, Riley."

Give into what? I thought to myself, even as a hand with dirt under too-long nails gripped the top of the door.

Laria's head appeared over the door as she levitated above me.

I squeezed my eyes closed, begged for some kind of guidance, and then unlocking the door, I kicked as hard as I could.

I raced out of the bathroom, and was immediately ripped back abruptly by someone. An elbow locked beneath my chin, and my feet were inches from touching the floor. I tried to fight back, but the arm tightened around my throat.

A little girl and her mom rounded the corner. The mom was yammering on the phone, but the little girl stared at me with wide eyes.

Randall abruptly dropped me onto the floor.

"What are you doing?" the woman asked, her tone borderline pissed off.

I straightened my shirt that had ridden up after Randall had yanked me back. "Nothing," I said, brushing my hair off my forehead with a trembling hand.

The woman and girl didn't move and even waited until I was past them before they continued down the hallway. I didn't make eye contact with anyone, and instead made a beeline for my friends.

Megan sat sandwiched between Milo and Cass, taking off her bowling shoes.

"Why did you leave me in the bathroom?" I asked Megan.

She looked up at me, her brows furrowed. "What do you mean? I walked out of the bathroom with you. We were together."

My mind was racing. "No, we didn't leave together. You left me."

"You're freaking me out, Ri," Megan said, standing. "You walked out of the stall, and we left the bathroom at the same time. When we got to the main room you said you were going to find Kade."

"It's true," Milo said. "When she came back, I asked where you were, and she said you went to find Kade."

I swallowed hard. "Where is Kade?"

"He went outside with Tom and Johan."

I bolted for the door.

"Riley, what's going on?" Megan called after me.

My mind was racing. Laria was masquerading as me again.

I ran out the door and nearly collided with an older couple who were walking in. "Sorry," I said under my breath.

"Riley." Kade stood with Johan and Tom, who crushed a cigarette beneath his heel. "Are you all right?"

I wanted to ask him if he'd seen "me" during the past five minutes. Hearing about the party at Tom's grandparents' cabin and knowing Laria had manipulated him into thinking it was me while I was away in Edinburgh was one thing, but to have her do it right under my nose—now *that* terrified me.

Chapter Sixteen

The entire ride home from the bowling alley, I remained quiet, my mind racing. I still couldn't shake what had happened in the bathroom, or the fact that Laria had masqueraded as me while I was in the same building.

And I was so exhausted. I felt so drained that the first thing I did when I got home was crawl into bed and take a nap.

I woke up to the sound of laughter. I glanced at the clock. Six thirty. I was surprised Miss Akin hadn't woken me up for dinner.

I washed my face, brushed my hair and my teeth, and then started down the stairs. I heard my family talking, and Miss A's laughter at something someone had said.

I walked into the living room and Dad looked up. "I was wondering if you fell in."

Fell in? "What do you mean?" I asked, noticing the empty chair with the nearly untouched plate sitting before it. "Who else is here?"

Dad frowned. "No one. Honey, that's your plate. You've been sitting here with us for the past thirty minutes...or until you went to the bathroom."

Dread filled every pore of my body.

"Dad, I've been asleep in my room since I got home from the bowling alley. I literally just now woke up."

He scratched his head. "You excused yourself from the table five minutes ago, Riley."

Shane set his fork down. "She's doing it again." At the bowling alley everyone had looked at me like I was crazy when I had said Laria was masquerading as me, until Shane had explained what was really going on. I hoped he could help me explain to Dad what was happening.

"What are you talking about?" I could see and hear Dad's exasperation as his gaze shifted between me and Shane.

Cheryl reached out and put a hand on his arm. "Hear them out."

For the first time I was grateful for Cheryl's presence.

"Dad, I'm completely serious. I've been asleep. I just now woke up and walked downstairs."

"Then who has been eating with us?" Miss Akin asked, shifting in her chair.

"Laria," I said.

Dad wiped his mouth with his napkin and tossed it onto his plate. "What the hell is everyone talking about?"

"We live in a haunted house, Dad," Shane said matter-of-factly. "Your daughter is being possessed by a malevolent spirit who is trying to kill her. If you were around more, maybe you would have grasped that a bit sooner."

Miss Akin glanced at Shane and shook her head, like she was telling him to save himself.

Dad puffed up and turned to Cheryl. "Perhaps you should retire to your room. I'll be along shortly."

She nodded, pressed the napkin to her lips, and left the room without looking back.

"I don't know what's happening here," Dad said, his voice barely above a whisper, "but I'm getting tired of it. If this is your way to somehow get attention—"

A door slammed somewhere in the house. I'd bet my life on it that it wasn't Cheryl because she didn't have enough time to get to the room she was staying in. Another door slammed, then another.

Seconds later Cheryl reappeared in the dining room doorway. "That wasn't me."

Dad tossed his napkin on the table. "Stay here," he said, leaving Cheryl little choice but to sit back down. Her eyes were enormous as she looked at me. It was pretty obvious that I made her nervous.

"Maybe I should go with him," Shane said, standing.

"Maybe you should stay here with us," Cheryl said, then bit her lip, like she had just overstepped her bounds.

Actually, I agreed with her. I didn't want Shane going anywhere.

A growling noise came from the far corner of the room.

Miss Akin picked up her butter knife and slowly turned.

"Do you by any chance own a dog I don't know about?" Cheryl asked, eyes wide, her back straight as a board.

Miss A shook her head.

Overhead we heard footsteps. And not just one set. People were walking back and forth, and there were multiple voices, like there were different conversations happening.

Shane met my gaze, and he whispered, "Son of a bitch."

Son of a bitch was right.

Although this was hardly the way I wanted validation, in a way I was glad that Dad was finally experiencing firsthand what we were going through. I wanted my dad to know that both Shane and I weren't nuts. Miss A knew the truth, and she believed us; hopefully now Dad would, as well.

Dad rushed into the room. "Was that a growl I heard?"

Shane nodded. "Yep."

The way Dad was looking at me, it was like I was causing drama on purpose.

I focused on him and even head-tapped him.

Sure enough, he thought I was responsible. He probably even thought that somehow I was making all this up to cause Cheryl to run and never look back.

I was crushed.

Above us the chandelier shook, so hard that the glass shades rattled. One even fell off the fixture and shattered on the table, shards of glass flying up and around us.

Cheryl screamed and Miss Akin looked ready to, but then got control of herself, and even put a reassuring hand on Cheryl's shoulder.

"This is what happens when you move into a three-hundred-year-old house," Shane said, and I knew he was going for humor, but Dad wasn't feeling it.

We lost the lights a second later.

Miss Akin gasped, or maybe it was Cheryl...or both.

"Calm down, everyone," Dad said, but I could tell by the quiver in his voice that he wasn't as cool and composed as he pretended to be.

"In the junk drawer there are candles and a lighter," Miss A said to no one in particular. It was clear she wasn't about to leave the room, though.

"I'll get it. Everyone just stay put." Dad walked out of the room and we all fell silent. There was a strange sense of expectation hanging in the air.

The sound of a chair being dragged across the wood floor could be heard, then a shriek. My hands gripped the sides of my own chair.

Dad rushed back in, holding a candle, his hand hovering above the flame. "What the hell is this?"

Cheryl was in the corner of the room, her back to us, facing the wall. Her head bowed down, her shoulders rising and falling as she took deep breaths.

"Who did this?" Dad said, his gaze looking from Shane and settling on me.

"Sir, the kids didn't move," Miss Akin said. "We're all still in our seats, and we never moved."

By his stunned expression, it was obvious he was trying to process what was happening. His mind was racing, trying to come up with a logical explanation.

"Do you believe us now?" Shane said.

Dad went to help Cheryl, who jumped when Dad put a hand on her shoulder.

"There's something here, Scott," Cheryl said. "They're not kidding. Whatever it was, it moved me effortlessly. I had no control at all, and whoever—or *whatever*—it was, had a lot of strength, because there was no struggle at all. And it was cold." She gave a shiver. "Like I was standing in a meat locker."

Dad watched her closely as she talked. Now that his girlfriend was telling him she believed us, maybe now he would finally believe too.

Shane yanked the candles out of the holders in the adjoining room and lit one for each of us.

"I think I put the torch under the kitchen sink," Miss Akin said.

Dad glanced at Shane. "Will you get the flashlight, Shane?"

"I'll go with you," I said, and we walked together out of the room.

I was relieved to get out of there, away from Dad's stare and Cheryl, who was watching me with a combination of fear and sympathy.

The second we were in the kitchen, Shane turned to me. "What the hell just happened in there?"

"This is getting out of control." I ran a hand through my hair. "How much worse can it get?"

"Don't say that."

Directly overhead we heard heavy footsteps.

Shane looked at me, brows lifted nearly to his hairline. "I bet Dad is thinking that Portland wouldn't be so bad right about now."

Portland didn't have Cheryl, though. If she stuck around after this, I'd have to give her props.

Something in the room moved. We both saw it, because Shane squinted into the darkness. "What the hell was that?"

I lifted the candle and every single cabinet door and drawer in the kitchen was wide open. The refrigerator door slowly swung open, the light casting a hazy glow into the kitchen. "How come the refrigerator light works but we've lost power?"

Or maybe spirits were turning lights on and off at will.

Shane grabbed my arm, and moved in front of me. "I don't know but let's get that flashlight."

The flashlight was right where Miss Akin said it would be, and Shane turned it on.

At the same time a hand pressed flat against my back.

"What's going on in there?" Dad yelled. He sounded furious.

A wave of dizziness washed over me, making me grab Shane. I fisted his T-shirt with one hand, and clenched the candle tight with the other.

Shadows were everywhere, and I felt them pushing closer. I heard my name being repeated over and over again, and it wasn't just one person, but many people talking over each other.

I started to sweat and experienced what felt like ants running all over my body. In fact, I expected to look down to see bugs crawling on me.

There was nothing.

Laria, Randall, and the others were trying to drive me crazy.

I stopped in mid-step and stared at the wavering candle in my hand, suddenly mesmerized by the golden flame. I brought the wick to my arm, craving the red-hot flame against my skin.

Shane glanced back at me. Eyes wide, he swatted the candle out of my hand. It flew across the kitchen and hit the window, where it extinguished. "What were you doing?"

I blinked a few times. "I don't know." But I did know. I had nearly burned myself. I had *wanted* to burn myself. I had wanted to hurt myself and experience that familiar sensation of pain.

My brother was terrified. I could see the concern in his eyes. We had both grown up a lot in the year since our mom had died, but the past months had made us grow up even more. We were different people now from when we had been when we arrived in Braemar.

Suddenly, the lights flickered and then went on.

"Thank God," Dad said from the dining room.

Miss Akin walked around the kitchen corner at the same time. Her gaze moved from Shane to me and back again. Shane walked over to the window and picked the candle off the sill. Miss A put her hand out. "I'll take those." She stopped short seeing the opened cupboards and drawers. "I think I'll be drinking some lavender tea tonight to settle my nerves. Anyone else care for a cup?"

Shane lifted his hand.

"Everything all right here?" Miss A asked, looking directly at me.

I nodded.

"We need to figure this out once and for all," Shane said, as he sat on a barstool and pushed the other one out for me.

"There must be a solution. We need peace in this home." Miss A put on a kettle of water, and Dad and Cheryl walked in a second later.

Cheryl's body language said it all. Her arms were crossed tightly across her body, and she struggled to make eye contact with me.

I wasn't about to tell Miss A that Shane and I were going to head into the hills to find Laria's grave in the hopes of binding her spirit.

Dad kept staring at me and Shane like he expected us to shout "surprise" at any time, and a film crew would walk out and announce he'd been the victim on a hidden camera show.

Miss A poured everyone a cup of tea, and we sat in silence, listening to the ticking of the clock on the wall. I normally didn't like tea, but Miss A swore by lavender to help calm her nerves.

As the minutes wore on and the lavender tea started kicking in, Dad sat down beside a silent Cheryl.

"Do we know of anyone who could come in and help us?" Dad finally said, breaking the awkward silence.

"You mean like an exorcist?" Shane asked, and Cheryl choked on her tea.

"I may know of someone who can help." Miss A was vigorously wiping down the counter. "I took the liberty of calling some people this past week. I found a Catholic priest out of Glasgow who comes in and does cleansings, but he's in London for a few weeks."

"Tell me he's discreet," Dad said under his breath, looking more than a little pissed that Miss Akin hadn't been forthcoming about what had been happening at the inn while he'd been away.

Shane shook his head, and opened his mouth, but I nudged his foot and he bit his bottom lip.

"He is well respected and comes highly recommended," Miss A added.

As they talked I knew that Laria and her friends were listening to every word. I would never underestimate the spirit world again. I knew the power they had, that once fear took hold of the victim or victims, that nearly anything was possible.

"Then it's settled," Dad said, like all was well. We'll get this matter cleared up and then hopefully life can get back to normal."

Get back to normal? What did he consider normal, I wondered.

From the corner of my eye I saw a flash out the window, a light in the distance, and then another and another, like lanterns coming toward us yet again. There were so many, close to a couple dozen, and every single time I blinked it was like they were suddenly ten feet closer, and then another ten feet closer.

"I think it's best if everyone heads to bed," Dad said. "It's been a long day and you have school tomorrow."

Miss A shifted on her feet. "I need to wash the dishes."

Cheryl immediately jumped into action and started clearing the dining room table. I met her in there. She watched me pretty closely, and I noticed her hands trembling. Was she actually scared of me? "I'm sorry you're going through so much."

"I'm not the only one going through it," I said, and wished I could take the words back when she blushed.

"Yes, of course."

When we returned to the kitchen, Dad was rinsing off dishes and handing them to Miss A to put into the dishwasher, and Shane was sweeping the floor.

There was an undercurrent of tension in the room, and I felt so much of it directed at me. I understood the fear. I'd been living with it for weeks now.

Chapter Seventeen

Shane crashed on the floor in my room. He lay on his back, arms folded beneath his head. "Maybe I should just bring my mattress in here."

"Or we could break through the wall and make it one big bedroom," I said sarcastically.

He barely cracked a smile. "I'm glad Miss Akin has someone who can help us."

Honestly, I was up for anything, even if it was a full-on Catholic exorcism. "We still need to bind Laria's grave, though."

I needed help...desperately. Tonight, I had wanted to burn myself, and those weren't my thoughts. Just like my behavior of late. I wasn't me. I knew that, and I sort of understood now the cases I'd read about for so long about how people had woken up from a dream to find that they'd done some weird, twisted, and sometimes, horrible things. I mean, my brother slept five feet away and I wondered if he was safe doing that. Thank God, I had Anne Marie and my mom, because if I didn't, I'd feel completely lost.

Shane fell off to sleep almost immediately, his soft snores filling the room.

I read for a while, said a protection prayer, and made an attempt at some relaxation visualization exercises that one of my books talked about, but I still couldn't sleep.

I rolled over onto my side and faced the door, and in the corner I swore I thought I saw someone standing there.

It wasn't Laria. It was too tall to be her. Too broad of shoulder.

My thoughts were confirmed when Randall stepped out of the darkness. A scream froze in my throat. There was no color to his eyes. Just the whites of his eyes was all I could see. His hands were out to his sides, facing upward, almost like he was praying to some force.

The sound of footsteps, like someone being dragged across the ceiling caught my attention. I glanced up. I blinked and then Laria was there, directly above me, her arms flung out to her sides, hair hanging down around her, eyes wide open, staring at me.

Shane. In my mind I had said my brother's name, but nothing came out.

Laria fell from the ceiling, dropping quickly toward me, and stopped inches from my body. It was like I was paralyzed. I couldn't move.

A slow smile spread across her face. In her hand she held a razor, and that razor dripped with blood. I glanced down and saw the gashes in my wrists at the same time I heard the cruel laughter. Blood was everywhere, pouring from the wounds onto my comforter, staining it bright red.

I grew more lightheaded by the second.

Laria turned and glanced to my right, and I realized too late that she was looking at Shane, who was still asleep on the floor beside my bed.

I opened my mouth, but when Laria glanced back at me, the scream died in my throat. I hit the headboard, right above where she'd etched the word 'DIE.'

Shane sat up abruptly. I expected him to see Laria or Randall, but it was obvious from his expression he didn't see anyone else...or my slashed wrists.

He frowned. "Can't you sleep?"

I closed my eyes for a few seconds, and when I opened them, Laria and Randall were gone. I glanced down at my wrists. There were no gashes. No blood. My heart thudded against my chest.

I sighed with relief, even as I realized that I was quickly coming undone.

"Riley, what's wrong?"

"I had a bad dream," I said, glancing at the clock. It was only just after two a.m., and it would be tough to get back to sleep.

"Maybe you should take one of those pills the doctor prescribed to you. They seemed to work and at least let you sleep."

As tempting as it was, I didn't want to be so medicated I couldn't help myself should the need arise. Plus, I always felt a little groggy the day after taking them. "I'm fine. Go back to sleep."

"You sure?" he asked, already pulling the comforter tighter around him.

I stayed awake for hours, and the last time I looked at the clock it was after four.

I entered the dining room, embarrassed to be late. The food had already been served, the smell reminding me that I had not eaten all day.

The family seemed not to notice my tardiness as they laughed at something Laird MacKinnon had said.

Seeing me, the men stood and waited as I took my seat.

Ian looked incredibly dashing in a white shirt, black breeches and knee-high boots. He had been out riding with his brother most the afternoon and still had a windswept look about him that nearly stole the breath from my lungs.

"Miss Murray, how lovely you look tonight," he said, his husky voice sending a delightful shiver up my spine.

I felt myself blush and grinned at him. I knew my emotions were there for all to see, and yet I did not care any longer. I loved Ian MacKinnon with all my heart and soul. I wanted to shout my happiness from the rooftops.

From the corner of my eye I saw Laria approach the table. I immediately sobered as she poured ale into Ian's goblet. Her hand trembled.

Ian took a long drink and set the goblet back down.

Conversation continued, and yet I noticed that something was not right with Ian. He placed a shaky hand on the table and blinked a few times in rapid succession.

Fear raced through me.

"Ian, what's wrong?" Lady MacKinnon asked, concern on her face as she looked at her son with alarm.

The blood seemed to drain from Ian's face.

Laird MacKinnon stood slowly. "Son, what is it?"

Duncan shot to his feet, knocking over a chair in his haste to get to his brother. He reached for the goblet, brought it to his nose. "Poison!" he roared, and all eyes turned toward Laria, who ran for the door.

I don't remember moving, and yet I was running away from the dining room, away from the horrible sight. Away from the panic and the screams that filled my ears.

In my room, I paced, hugging my arms to my body, not sure what to do when a terrible wail filled the castle.

The breath froze in my lungs. I knew what that cry meant.

Lady MacKinnon mourned for her beautiful son.

Chaos ensued.

There was screaming, yelling, and a commotion in the stairwell.

The sounds continued out into the castle courtyard. I watched it all from my bedroom window. Laria was screaming. That bloodcurdling shrill made the hair on my arms stand on end.

The family wanted blood, and they were seeking their own vengeance.

Laria's father pleaded with the family to be lenient, to put her in the dungeon, to send her away, but they would not hear of it.

The noose was thrown over the tree branch, and Duncan tested it, making sure it would not break.

Laria kicked her captors, in an effort to escape one last time.

I turned away, unable to look any longer.

"Margot."

I flinched, glancing over my shoulder and scanning the room. I had clearly heard my name being whispered in my ear. My God, that voice had sounded so much like Ian's.

A woman's scream pierced the night, and then there was silence.

When I next looked out the window, I saw the small group of men, along with a horse and a body flung over its back, making their way toward the river.

I gripped tight to the window frame, unable to believe I was caught up in such events. Even more, I found it impossible to accept that the beautiful young man I had met and fallen in love with was dead.

Chapter Eighteen

I gave myself a final once-over in the mirror. Cass's step-mom had hired a cosmetologist to come in and do makeup and hair for the party. I stared at my reflection and barely recognized the girl with the haunted, smoky eyes. I normally didn't wear a lot of makeup, and I never put so much effort into my hair. The stylist had done an intricate updo and she'd put a gloss on it that made the blonde strands shine. The cobalt blue dress cut in the Grecian goddess style did wonders for my pale skin tone, but also made the dark circles beneath my eyes more obvious.

For the past week I'd had the same dream about Ian's death. Every single night. No matter what, I always woke up in the same place, and I always felt a sickening sensation...like I was just waiting for Laria to show up.

But she was surprisingly absent, as was Peter and even the blonde woman who had appeared from time to time.

I felt like it was the calm before the storm.

At school this week, three of my teachers had asked me to stay after class, and each repeatedly asked if everything was okay at home because I'd been quiet and withdrawn. I was agitated and pissed off, tired and sleep deprived, but it's not like I could explain that to my teachers.

Kade and I had even gotten into a stupid argument last night. It was ridiculous, over him being five minutes late. All evening he kept asking me if I was all right. I was sick of everyone asking me if I was all right.

Thank God my dad had left for Edinburgh to spend the weekend with Cheryl. I'd told him that the activity in the house had calmed down, and he seemed relieved. So relieved he had left us alone, which still kind of stung. Given what had been happening, my mom would have never let us stay by ourselves, but Dad figured we had Miss Akin, and that she would call if we needed him.

This morning when I woke up, I considered not going to the party, but Megan, apparently sensing that I was going to bail, had put the brakes on that. She'd picked me up and from the second we got to Cass's, I was getting sucked into the whole party theme. It was going to be fun, and Cass's dad had gone out of his way to make her day special.

The party was set up in the basement, and already the DJ was playing techno music; our steps all fell into rhythm with the beat.

Megan wore a cute red dress with a plunging neckline, and Cait a black dress with feathers on the skirt and a halter top that showed off her athletic back. Cass, not to be outdone, wore a long, shimmering gold dress that was red carpet ready. She looked amazing, and much older than a seventeen-year-old girl.

The DJ announced her, and a loud cheer went up. I recognized a lot of people from school, and a few faces I didn't know at all. I lingered back from the spotlight with Cait, and Megan waited as Cass posed a few seconds at the bottom step to take it all in. I had to admit that Cass's stepmum, better known as Bitchzilla, had done a great job on the decorating, or hiring the event planner, because the place was off the chain. Stars glimmered on the dark ceiling, and a disco ball twirled over the black and white checkerboard dance floor.

"This is sick," Cait said, huge smile in place.

I nodded in agreement. I was happy to be part of this night, to have found this group of girls, and to have been accepted into their circle.

The party at Cass's was in full swing by the time Kade showed up with Johan and Tom. I saw him over the heads of the others, and as he came walking toward me I felt a sense of pride. Pride that he was mine. That he had stuck by my side. That no matter what, we were going to stay together.

He was dressed in a long-sleeved slim-fitting black shirt and dark jeans. His hair had gotten longish and I liked how the strands curled up at the collar.

"You look amazing," he said, pulling me in for a kiss.

I grinned, pleased by the compliment. "So do you."

"Look at that," he said motioning toward a group of girls who were pouring a bottle of vodka into the punchbowl when Bitchzilla wasn't looking.

It was bound to be a wild night.

I was excited for Cass. I knew how much she wanted to drive. When her dad came down the stairs and asked everyone to head to the driveway, she was all smiles.

Cass had already practiced her surprise face in the mirror when we were getting ready in her suite of a room, and I had my camera ready to capture the moment. Kade's fingers tightened on mine as we walked outside.

Cass's dad was tall and barrel-chested, with a grey comb-over and a penchant for wearing cowboy boots and jeans. He walked behind her, hands over her eyes, and signaled for everyone to count to three. Down the driveway, headlights turned on. Everyone cheered as a brand new pearl white BMW rolled up the cobbled drive, chrome wheels shimmering.

I have to admit, Cass did herself proud with the over-the-top reaction, even managing some tears. Who knew, maybe they weren't all for show. After all, she had wanted a Beamer.

I met Megan and Cait's gazes and we all shared a smile, happy for our friend, and knowing that we were going to enjoy the perks of that car as well. "Score," Megan said under her breath. "She can drive now, and use Daddy's gas card while she's at it."

I had little doubt Cass would be driving from here on out.

While Cass and her father took the BMW for a quick spin, we were all ushered back inside by Bitchzilla. I was stunned, not to mention extremely irritated when I saw Dana in the crowd.

"How the hell did she sneak in here?" Megan asked.

Cait shook her head. "I'm sure she snuck in when we were all occupied with the big reveal." She didn't hesitate and walked straight over to her. They talked for a few minutes, Dana glancing past Cait's shoulder toward me. Shaking her head, Cait headed back toward me. "Seems her mum is an acquaintance of Bitchzilla's."

"But this is Cass's party," Megan said, stating the obvious.

"Maybe Cass will tell her to leave," Cait said, sounding hopeful.

Or maybe I would just have to finally deal with her...and her friends.

Kade was talking with Johan, Tom, and a kid I had seen around school.

"I'm going inside with the girls," I said.

"I'll be right there," Kade replied, and I felt his gaze on me as I walked away. I glanced over my shoulder and sure enough he was watching me. I flashed a smile and he winked.

I followed the girls into the bathroom where we spent the next ten minutes reapplying makeup. I didn't pretend that Dana being here didn't bother me. I couldn't stand her, and she would forever be a constant reminder of what Laria had done to Kade that night at Tom's house.

I left the bathroom before the other girls, and walked down the hallway. Kade headed my way, his lips spreading into a devilish grin. "Hey, you want to dance?"

I was surprised he was asking. I guess I never took him as the dancing type, but I was happy he was. Having taken dance classes for years when I was younger, I loved any opportunity to dance.

Half the guests were already out on the floor, moving and gyrating to a song with a great beat.

Kade took me by the hand and I followed him out to the dance floor, near the middle of the crowd. He was an incredible dancer, and I could feel the blood in my veins sizzle as he moved closer. The heat came off him in waves. His hand slid to my hip.

I reached up and touched his arm.

The side of his mouth curved in a sexy smile, and he leaned and whispered in my ear, "I want to be with you tonight."

My breath caught in my throat. "I want to be with you, too."

Despite all the drama of late, I wanted to be alone with him. The day at the river seemed like a lifetime ago and I craved the intimacy we'd shared that day.

I saw Dana dancing with a friend, and the way they both watched us, with huge smiles on their faces, made me frown and wonder what she was up to now. I quickly looked away. I would not let that bitch ruin my night.

"You're a great dancer," Kade said in my ear. "So sexy."

"You're pretty damn good yourself," I said, feeling slightly light-headed. I'd had a cup of the spiked punch, maybe enough to get a little buzz on, but not enough to get drunk and pass out.

At least I was in good hands.

The dizziness faded. We moved closer together, and I slipped my arms around his neck. He slid his hands around my waist, and held me so close I could feel his heart pounding against my chest.

His hands moved from my hips to my butt.

I lifted a brow. He lowered his head, his lips hovering over mine.

A second later Kade was ripped away, and before I could blink Johan was on the floor and Kade was on top of him, punching him in the face.

What the hell?

It took Shane, Tom, and Milo to pull Kade off of Johan.

Johan's face was bloodied, and Kade's chest was rising and falling as he looked at Johan, then at me.

Cass's eyes narrowed as she watched me. "What the fuck, Riley?" She rushed off the floor and I glanced at Megan, who shook her head and ran after Cass.

Everyone was staring at me, mostly in surprise. My heart was a roar in my ears. Something was very wrong.

Shane came up to me and put his arm around me. "You okay?"

"No, not really." I was ready to ask him what had happened when Kade came up to me, took me by the hand and walked off the floor.

"Dude, where are you going?" Shane said, right behind us.

Kade turned on him. "Give me a minute with your sister, will you? She'll be fine. I promise."

"She better be," Shane replied, and glanced at me. "You okay? If you want to leave, we can go right now."

"I'm fine," I said, and followed Kade, whose fingers tightened on mine.

We walked out the back door, onto a beautiful patio, and past guests who went silent the second they saw us. I had to take two steps to his one. I could feel his rage.

We rounded the corner, and up a walkway on the side of the house. He abruptly dropped my hand and turned on me. "Why would you dance with Johan like that? I know we fought last night, and you've been distant this week, but I don't—"

"What do you mean dancing with Johan?" I said, dread filling me at his words. "I was dancing with you."

He watched me for a long minute and shook his head. "What?"

"Kade, I swear on my life that I was dancing with you. I wasn't dancing with Johan."

His eyes narrowed. "I don't understand."

Oh my God, no wonder Cass was so mad. She had seen me dancing with Johan. *Everyone* had seen me dancing—and more—with Johan. Laria was at it again…

He ran a trembling hand through his hair. "Wait, you're telling me you thought you were dancing with me?"

"I *was* dancing with you. Seriously, go ask Johan—ask him if he remembers any of the past ten minutes. I guarantee you he won't remember a thing."

"This sounds familiar," he said, shaking his head. "Bloody hell, when will she stop?"

"Hopefully when we bind her to her grave," I said absently, my mind racing. I needed to find Cass and explain. This looked really bad. "I should find Cass and Megan, and you should probably talk to Johan."

His fingers threaded through mine. "Let's go together."

I nodded, but he stopped short and pulled me close. "I'm sorry, Riley. I just saw red when I saw you together. I couldn't believe my eyes."

I cradled his face between my palms. "I love you, Kade. I would never knowingly hurt you. I want you. I don't want anyone else."

He looked so relieved. He kissed me softly. "I love you, too...and I don't want anyone else either."

We hadn't made it five feet into the house when Cass's stepmum blocked us from coming inside.

"It's time for you to leave," she said, looking at Kade. She glanced at our linked hands and lifted a brow.

Shane and Cait came up to us.

"I need to go," Kade said, looking at his sister. "Will you tell Johan I'd like to talk to him outside?"

Cait nodded. "Do you want me to come with you?"

"No, that's okay. You stay and have fun with your friends. I'm sure Cass or Megan will drive you home."

There was no way I was staying at the party. "I'm coming with you."

He didn't argue with me.

"I just need to get my purse," I said to Cass's stepmum, who let me in, but she made a point of keeping Kade out.

"I'll meet you out front," Kade said, and I nodded and raced up the steps to Cass's room where I'd left my things.

Cass and Megan were in the room and seeing me, Cass looked at me, eyes red and swollen. "What the fuck was that, Riley? I thought you were my friend."

"Laria's back. I swear to God I was dancing with Kade. That wasn't Johan. I didn't even see Johan until Kade had him on the floor."

"Fuckin' hell," Megan said, getting up from where she'd been sitting on the bed. "I knew something was off. I just knew there was no way you would do that to Kade or Cass."

"I'm sorry, Cass. I didn't mean to mess up your birthday."

Cass swallowed hard and gave me a hug. "I feel like such an idiot."

"*I* feel like an idiot," I said. "All those people out there saw me dancing with Johan." I just wanted to leave, go home with Kade, and forget about tonight.

"They probably just think you're getting back at Kade for what happened at Tom's party," Megan said, and then clamped her mouth shut. "Sorry, I didn't mean it like that."

"That's okay, and I'm sure you're right."

I grabbed my purse, gave Cass a hug. "Your stepmum asked Kade to leave, and I really need to go with him."

She opened her mouth to argue, but Megan interrupted. "I completely understand. If it was Milo, I'd do the same. You two have a good night."

"I could talk to my stepmum and see if she'd reconsider," Cass said, already heading for the door.

"You know what—I think it's time for us to go, especially considering Laria is here. Let's face it, who knows what else she'll pull if I stay."

Cass's eyes went wide.

"Let us at least walk you out," Megan said, beating me to the door.

I nodded and followed behind them, relieved things were okay between us.

The party had resumed, and aside from a few gawkers, no one paid us much attention.

Outside, Kade was talking to Johan, with Tom, Shane, Cait, Milo and Richie nearby.

I breathed a sigh of relief. Johan nodded at something Kade said. Kade put his hand out and Johan took it.

"Thank God," Megan said under her breath.

I couldn't agree more.

Dana walked up to Kade and he turned around. He frowned at her, and she slapped him across the face.

Oh shit. I rushed toward them.

"What about us?" she said, shrieking.

"There is no us, Dana," Kade said, sounding exhausted. "There never was."

"That's not what you said the night of Tom's party."

I cleared my throat and she turned around, her gaze shifting slowly over me. "She wants Johan, anyway. We all saw them practically shagging on the dance floor before you busted them."

My cheeks grew hot as others gathered around us.

"You fucking asshole," Dana yelled.

People filed out onto the yard, obviously wanting to get a glimpse of the train wreck.

Dana was pounding on Kade's chest, and screeching like a banshee, tears streaming down her face.

Johan stepped between them and held Dana at bay.

In that moment, all the anger, frustration, and jealousy I'd felt toward Dana hit me hard. I wanted to rip her eyes out.

"I can't believe you want that freak!" she screamed.

"Dana, get the hell out," Cass said, furious. "Riley and Kade are my friends, and they were actually invited to this party. You weren't."

Dana turned to her buddies, almost like she expected them to do something.

"I left my purse inside," one of them said.

"Well, go get it," Megan replied, pointing toward the house.

"Okay. Jesus," she said with a sneer. "You don't have to be such a bitch."

I glanced up and I saw the faces of the others amongst the crowd of school friends. I blinked a few times, but those faces didn't shift or change back. When I glanced at Dana, I saw Laria's features juxtaposed over hers.

Kade's fingers slid around mine. "Are you ready?"

I nodded.

"I can't believe you want the cutter over me," Dana said, her voice odd. All my friends heard it because they had the same shocked expressions on their faces.

An unexplainable rage rushed through me. I didn't even remember moving, but the next thing I knew, I was standing in front of Dana and I punched her hard.

Dana lifted her hand to hit me back, but I caught her wrist.

"You touch me and I'll kill you." The words came from me, but they didn't sound like me.

Dana's eyes widened. "Whatever...*bitch*."

I had never touched anyone before, and yet I lost my mind in that moment as I saw red.

Chapter Nineteen

Kade lay on my bed beside me, his fingers lazily drawing circles on my arm. It had been too long since we'd last just relaxed together. I could have stayed like this forever. The past weeks had been traumatic for our relationship, and I could feel him holding onto me with both hands, especially after tonight's nightmare.

Having the shoe on the other foot, so to speak, definitely put things in perspective. Now I knew firsthand what Kade had experienced at Tom's party, because tonight when I'd been dancing, I'd been with Kade, not Johan.

I was just so happy Kade was able to talk to Johan before we'd left, but I was still stewing about Dana's outburst.

Kade was bothered by it, too. His thoughts were so chaotic.

Poor Cass, Megan, and Cait. Little had they realized what havoc I would cause in their lives when they had befriended me.

I knew with all that was happening, I shouldn't involve anyone else, but I needed Kade's strength more than ever. And as much as Laria was trying to come between us, I knew that we were meant to be together.

"You sure Miss A is asleep?" Kade said, pulling me closer.

"Trust me, she sleeps like the dead."

His eyes widened. "That's hardly reassuring considering..."

I smiled, glad he still had a sense of humor.

I pressed my lips against his jaw, kissing a pathway down his neck, the pulse there quickening.

His hands were at my back, unzipping my dress. "I've missed you, Riley."

"I've missed you, too." It had been weeks since the day he'd taken my virginity, and I wanted him, needed to feel his hands on my body, touch his body in turn, and experience the shared excitement that seemed to vibrate through my very core.

I unbuttoned his shirt, and pushed it off his shoulders. He sat up and slid it off, and helped me off with my dress.

There was a heavy-lidded look to his eyes I recognized that made the blood in my veins simmer.

I unbuckled his belt, unbuttoned his jeans, and slid the zipper down. I pressed a kiss against his chiseled abdomen, the muscles there clenching beneath my lips.

With a little growl, he flipped me onto my back, and as I stared up into those beautiful blue eyes, all my concerns and fears evaporated.

My arms slid around his neck and I lifted my head for a kiss.

He didn't disappoint, kissing me softly at first, but then with a fiery need that matched my own.

I rested my head against Kade's shoulder and fought to catch my breath. I felt exhilarated, and I marveled at how naturally our bodies fit together, how we had moved together so perfectly.

A long finger slid along my spine, upward, along the base of my neck, and then back down again.

I smiled, happy and relaxed for the first time in weeks. I was finally able to just let everything go. "What's so funny?" he asked, arching a brow, a soft smile on his lips.

"I'm happy and content," I said.

He kissed my shoulder, and wound a lock of my hair around his finger. "I am, too."

I noticed two of the fingers on his right hand were cut.

"You're hurt."

His brows lifted. "That's what I get for punching my best friend in the face."

"You know, if we make it through this, we'll make it through anything."

I put my hand up to his and he wove his fingers through mine, and kissed the top of my hand. "Can I ask you something?"

"Sure."

"Do you remember a few weeks ago when you told me about a dream you'd had where we were in the castle looking for a book?" I recalled how shocked I'd been when he'd told me, especially since Ian and I had broken into the castle weeks before to find Laria's journal.

He nodded. "Yes."

"That actually happened. We—the two of us—were looking for a journal."

His eyes narrowed as he watched me. "I don't understand."

Maybe now hadn't been the time to talk about his past life as Ian, but I'd brought it up, so I was committed. "What if I told you that you and Ian were the same person? That it was me and Ian who looked for the journal."

"But you said that you and Ian hung out this summer after you moved here. If I'm supposed to be him..."

"I don't understand how it works, exactly...I just know what Ian told me and what I've been told by Anne Marie."

"Anne Marie who is now dead?" He frowned. "Did she tell you this when she was alive?"

I chewed on my lip. Why the hell had I opened my big mouth? I knew this could go sideways on me fast...and I was slowly leaning toward the point of no return.

"That's a lot to wrap the brain around."

It was. I knew that. "Even a lot of your mannerisms are the same," I said, reaching for the drawer in my nightstand where I had stashed the pictures I had drawn of Ian and Kade. The one of Kade had been crushed in my fist when I'd first heard about him and Dana. I had kept it in a book to straighten it out and it had helped, but it still seemed pretty obvious I had intentionally crumpled it. "I drew this picture one night. Just look at the similarities. Even the way you're sitting."

His gaze shifted back and forth between the pictures. "Look at the way he's looking at you." It was funny, because he actually sounded jealous.

"We had an instant connection, but now it makes even more sense."

"He told you that he was me?"

"Yes, after he died. He has come to me in my dreams. I keep seeing a life we had experienced together when Laria was alive." Even hearing myself say it aloud made me cringe. As I kept talking about that lifetime, what I had seen, and how Laria had been, he listened intently.

He asked me a good twenty questions about Ian, and not once did he make me feel like I was crazy.

"It actually makes sense," he finally said. "I know it sounds strange."

I laughed, because nothing sounded strange to me any longer.

"I've always been so drawn to the pictures of him and his family. More so than any other of my other ancestors' pictures."

I breathed a sigh of relief, grateful he now knew everything.

His phone rang, and he glanced at the screen. "It's my mum. I didn't realize how late it was." He gave me a kiss, and started getting dressed.

I did the same, and walked him to the front door.

"Will you go to Inverness with me and my family tomorrow?" he asked, one hand on the door handle. "We're meeting family up there for my cousin's tenth birthday."

"I wish I could, but I have a homework assignment I need to get finished." I knew if I showed up in class without it, Mr. Monahan would keep me after school for detention, and that's the last thing I needed right now.

"I'll help you with the assignment on the way."

It was pretty clear that he wasn't going to take no for an answer. Plus, I could think of worse things than hanging out with his family for the afternoon.

Maddy was unusually quiet on the drive to Inverness the next day. She was playing a game on her iPod, while watching me under lowered lids. She'd been acting a little shady and I didn't like it.

Cait was quiet and obviously hung over. She wore sunglasses and the sun wasn't even out.

The silence in the car allowed me to finish my homework. As promised, Kade helped me.

When we got to the pizza parlor, the place was slammed with people. Kade's extended family was very nice, but I was bothered by Maddy's cool demeanor toward me. When she slid away to the arcade, I excused myself and found her playing a video game.

"What's up, Maddy?" I asked.

She shrugged. "Not much."

"You've been quiet today. Is something wrong?"

"Not really," she said defensively.

Her video game ended. She took a deep breath and turned to look at me. "Hanway says Laria is possessing you."

Hearing those words out of anyone's mouth was disconcerting, but it was especially horrifying coming out of a twelve-year-old's mouth. Particularly a psychic twelve-year-old.

"Possessing me?"

"Remember the football game, and how Laria and those hooded guys came after you? You were possessed then. Do you have moments where you have a tough time remembering..."

"Yes."

"Again, possessed." She took a deep breath, released it. "What about your dreams?"

"I'm having the same dream every night."

"About a past life you had with Ian...and the witch, right?"

I swallowed hard. "Yes."

She glanced over her shoulder, and looked around, like she was terrified to even be caught talking to me. "I'm afraid for you, Riley. I mean, I'm *really* afraid. This isn't good. She's so dangerous, and Hanway says she could end up killing you if she wants to."

Is that what Laria wanted? I wondered. Did she really want to kill me, or did she just want to make me suffer? Now that I'd been experiencing life as Margot, and I knew what I had been to Ian in that lifetime, it made sense that she was trying to finish the job she had started back then...but would she know my dreams? Would she have figured out that past life link to Ian, or was she just mad at me for helping Ian cross over? Or was it a combination of everything?

"She won't kill me," I said, hoping to ease her fears.

"Hanway said he watched you walking in the cemetery night before last...like at two in the morning."

Hanway was losing it, because I hadn't been walking in the cemetery, especially at two in the morning.

"You wore an orange T-shirt and black pants."

My mind raced. Oh my God. I had worn my dad's old ratty orange Harley T-shirt and a pair of black yoga pants to bed the other night. How the hell had Hanway known that, especially since he never left the castle...unless he had actually seen me?

But you could clearly see the cemetery from the castle.

I felt the blood drain from my face. Come to think of it, I had woken up that following morning and was mystified why the bottom of my yoga pants had been damp.

"You need to focus more on protecting yourself against spirits."

"I'm protecting myself. I've followed the books I've read to the letter."

"It's not enough. You need to do more...because she's gotten into your head."

She was doing more than getting into my head.

I saw Kade approach. "The pizzas are ready."

"Good, I'm starved," Maddy said, and glanced at me. "You coming?"

I picked at my pizza and tried to engage with Kade's family as much as possible, but I couldn't get what Maddy had said out of my mind, especially about Hanway seeing me walk through the cemetery at night. Shane was crashing in my room. Wouldn't he have heard me leave, or was Laria somehow manipulating him too?

I couldn't put anything past her.

Chapter Twenty

I was checking the answers on my homework assignment for the third time when I heard a clicking sound from outside in the hallway. I also heard voices, like a group of people were talking. I knew Shane had left with Richie and Milo after dinner. He'd said he'd be home by nine.

I checked the bedside clock. It was quarter 'til.

Maybe Miss A just had her television on really loud.

I tried to focus on my assignment when the voices grew louder. I set my book aside, went to the door, and opened it. Miss Akin's door was shut. I knew she crashed at nine o'clock. I walked toward her room and listened for any sounds. I didn't hear a television.

The unmistakable feeling of being watched made me turn. From the corner of my eye I caught sight of a woman with light-colored hair, and once again I heard voices. Had it been the lady I'd seen sacrificed in the woods? I wondered why she would show herself now when she'd been so scarce lately.

I needed to go to my room and stay there until Shane got home. I was anxious to tell him what Maddy had told me about walking in the cemetery. I could tell him what I had just now seen and we could investigate together.

Walking back down the hall, I quickly passed by the staircase and went into my room. I started to shut the door when I heard children giggling.

I stepped back into the hallway. A million different reasons why I should stop came to mind as I took a left and walked slowly toward the sounds. I couldn't stop from putting one foot in front of the other. The giggles came again, louder this time, and from the last door on the left, a room that was used to stockpile my dad's computer equipment.

I opened the door and walked in. The boxes were stacked six feet high, and in the corner there was a door to what looked to be a closet.

"What am I doing?" I said under my breath, and turned when something moved past me, the scent of vanilla so strong. My heart missed a beat. It smelled like my mom.

The blonde woman walked in, looked at me, then turned and walked through the door of the closet.

I felt the unexplainable urge to follow her.

I opened the closet, and there was a steep staircase of about twenty steps.

Come.

The next thing I knew, I was standing in a small attic room.

How in the hell had I ever gotten up here? I didn't remember walking up the steps.

No light guided my way, and yet I didn't feel fear—just a strange pull. Even though it was dark, I seemed to know where I was going...

Hurry. The single word made my heart miss a beat.

I frowned. Had that been my mom's voice I'd heard?

The now familiar sensation of being slightly dizzy filled me, but I fought through it. Out of the blackness, I saw a light filtering in beneath the doorway. A light from where?

I pushed the door open easily, a creak following its movement.

A gust of wind whipped my hair and drops of rain pelted my cheek. The door led outside? Up to the roof, to be precise. A small flat landing that looked out over the town.

My mom stood with her back toward me.

"Mom," I said, taking a step closer to her, desperate to feel her loving arms around me.

I heard my name being called from what sounded like far away.

"Riley, do you hear me?"

I opened my eyes, blinked, and found myself staring into the blue eyes of my brother. I could see the concern on his face. He leaned down, hands on my shoulders, face inches from mine. "Riley, you need to fight her. You can't let her win."

What the hell was he talking about?

In the hallway, just beyond his shoulder I saw Miss Akin talking with Milo and Richie. Miss A dabbed at her eyes with a tissue. Every one of them looked terrified, making me wonder what had happened.

The last thing I remembered was working on my homework.

"What's going on?" I asked, noticing for the first time my wet hair.

The clothes I'd worn earlier were tossed on the floor in a pile, and I had on sweats and a black tank top.

Shane opened his mouth, then closed it as quickly. "You don't remember?"

"I was doing my homework." Whatever had happened, had been enough to scare everybody.

"Who's Peter?" he asked.

"Peter's the spirit of a little boy I met at the school." He was making me really nervous. "Why?"

"Right before you were ready to jump off the roof...you looked back over your shoulder and you said his name. Then you were yanked back so hard, you ended up on your ass like ten feet away from where you'd been standing."

Chills rushed up my spine.

"I mean, we all saw it." Shane ran a trembling hand through his hair. "Didn't we guys?"

"Yeah," Milo and Richie said in unison.

My heart was pounding so loud it was a roar in my ears. "Jump off the roof? I wasn't even on the roof."

"Riley, when we pulled up to the inn, you were standing on the very edge of the roof, staring straight ahead. We were screaming your name but it's like you didn't hear us. You were somewhere—or someone—else."

Milo shifted on his feet. "Ri, he's telling you the truth. This is insane. Bloody hell, if I hadn't of seen it with my own eyes, I wouldn't believe it."

"I gotta get home," Richie said to Milo. He couldn't even make eye contact with me. "I was supposed to be home thirty minutes ago."

"I'll take you right now," Milo said, then glanced at Shane. "I can stay over if you need me to. I don't mind, honestly..."

"Thanks," Shane said absently. "But it's probably best you go home now anyway."

Milo actually looked relieved. "I'm glad you're okay, Ri," he said, yanking Richie by the arm.

They were out of the house in seconds.

My mind was racing. How could I have almost jumped off the roof, and yet I couldn't remember anything?

A shiver rushed through me. Kind of like I didn't remember walking through the cemetery the other night either, but Hanway had seen me, and now tonight my brother and his friends had, as well.

And I had absolutely zero recollection.

There was no denying that Laria *was* possessing me.

"You're under a spiritual attack," Miss Akin said matter-of-factly.

I swallowed past the lump in my throat. "I never thought it would get to this point." I honestly had thought I would be stronger than Laria, and that I would be well aware of what was happening if she did take me over.

I thought back to when Shane had been possessed, how tormented he'd been by the things his friends had told him. I so understood how he felt. What else had she done that I wasn't aware of? I was terrified to learn the whole truth.

Shane glanced at Miss A. "Will you watch her? I'm going to call Kade and see if he can come over for a while."

I didn't argue with him. I needed to see Kade's face...to hear his reassurance.

"I'll call him, my dear. You stay with your sister. Can I get you anything?" Miss A asked, lingering at the door.

"Maybe a cup of lavender tea."

She nodded. "You got it," she said, closing the door behind her.

The second the door was closed, Shane looked me in the eye. "Riley, you have to do everything you can to push her away. She has a serious foothold on you. You would have died tonight if it hadn't been for Peter."

I have no idea why I laughed, but I did, the sound surprising me.

It surprised Shane, too. He sat back on his heels, his brows furrowed into a frown.

Horrible thoughts abruptly flashed through my mind. I heard the words *"Do it,"* seconds before I grabbed Shane around the neck and started choking him.

"Do it. Do it. Do it." The words repeated over and over again in my ears.

Shane's eyes widened in shock. He grabbed my hands and pulled hard, his face turning red with the effort that it took to break free. Normally, he was much stronger than I was, but I felt like I had the strength of ten men inside me.

Chapter Twenty-One

I heard the clock ticking on the wall. I slowly opened my eyes. I was still on the bed, but now Shane was on his knees and he was crying, tears falling, leaving wet marks on his T-shirt. He sniffed and released a breath.

I tried to move, but I couldn't. Not even a fraction. I remembered both Megan and Shane saying that they were held down by an invisible force. That's exactly what was now happening to me.

"Mom, help us," Shane whispered. "God, or whoever is up there. *Please...*" This last came out on a groan.

Even when Mom had died, I hadn't seen him this distraught and it rocked me to the core. I wanted to reach out to him, to say something, to try and reassure him as best I could...but invisible hands continued to hold me down. I couldn't even speak.

An intense laughter vibrated throughout the room.

Apparently Shane could hear the laughter as well, because he clamped his hands over his ears.

Minutes later, with the laughter still lingering in the room, his shoulders sagged. Slowly his head fell back on his shoulders and he stared at the ceiling, palms turned up. "God, do something, damn it. Prove that you're here, because I am five seconds to losing what little faith I do have."

I could tell he held his breath...as he waited for something. For a sign, for someone to come and rescue us. The minutes crept by so slowly, and still I couldn't move.

Shane's jaw clenched tight, his hands tightening into fists at his sides. "I am on my *fucking* knees and I am begging you for help."

I felt his anguish, his frustration, his fear, his anger—all rolled into one wave of despair—and I could do nothing. Tears rolled down my face, into my hair.

A low, guttural moan sounded from him. I felt that cry tear all the way to my soul.

Like Shane, I prayed for help.

Slowly he stood, and with a primal yell, swiped the lamp from the table and threw it against the wall. "Where the fuck are you?"

I heard footsteps on the stairs, and then Kade rushed into the room, and Miss A was right behind him.

He took everything in on a glance. "What's happening?" he asked at the same time my upper body came up off the bed, vertically without any effort from me. Kade, Shane, and Miss A's eyes went wide. From their expressions, the movement must have looked as bizarre as it felt.

I was pushed back a second later...hard, and then lifted up again in the same fluid motion.

Kade was beside me a second later. "Why is her nose bleeding?" He swiped the blood with his thumb. The blood flowed over my lips and I had to blow out to keep from swallowing it.

"I called a local shaman who is on his way," Miss A said from near the door. "He should be here any minute. Hang in there, Riley."

It actually helped me from gagging on my own blood when my upper body lifted off the bed again, but this time I was yanked right back down, only to be hauled up again.

Kade tried to hold onto me, but he was thrown across the room, and hit the wall with a sickening thud.

"Stop it!" I screamed, relieved when I could finally push the words past my lips.

Kade scrambled to his feet and came back toward me, but was immediately thrown against the wall again.

I barely had time to catch a breath before I was lifted up again and slammed back down again.

"*You belong to us now,*" I heard the words plainly, seconds before the room went black.

Chapter Twenty-Two

When I opened my eyes, I saw a man about sixty years old staring down at me. "Hello, Riley, my name is Angus, and this," he said, pointing to a short, plump woman, "is my wife, Dot. She is my helper, and also has the gift of second sight."

Kade sat beside me, holding my hand, Miss A was at the foot of the bed, and Shane was on the phone.

"Here you go," Shane said, handing the phone to Angus.

"I have your permission then, Mr. Williams?" Angus said. "All right, thank you. Yes, indeed, I will. Thank you, sir."

Angus handed the phone to me.

I swallowed hard. "Hello?"

"Riley, I'm on my way home," my dad said. "Angus and Dot know what they're doing, and I have entrusted them to help you. You'll be okay, sweetheart."

Hearing his voice brought me relief. "Okay." My voice cracked. "I'll see you soon." I handed the phone to Shane, who squeezed my shoulder and walked into the hallway.

"It's okay," Kade said, brushing his free hand over my forehead. "Soon all of this will be a memory."

I was so nervous. Actually, I was terrified, and I couldn't explain the many emotions rushing through me.

"Let's begin," Angus said, and I saw Shane step back into the room. He was still on the phone, so apparently Dad wanted a play-by-play on what was happening.

Angus placed crystals on my forehead, and then on certain points of my body.

Immediately I heard a loud growling in my ears. Beads of sweat rolled off my forehead onto the comforter. I felt deeply depressed... like when Mom had died. The feelings rocked me, and I started to cry uncontrollably.

"You're all right, Riley," Kade said reassuringly. I could hear the strain in his voice.

"It is completely normal for the victim to experience different emotions of the spirit," Dot explained.

I began trembling, and heard a voice calling to me. At first it sounded right next to my ear, then far away. It was so bizarre, and completely disorienting.

"Riley, is the one who is haunting you here?" Angus asked.

I nodded, knowing the reason behind my sudden depression. I hadn't expected such a deep sadness from Laria.

Angus poured oil into his palm, dipped his finger in, and proceeded to draw a line from my forehead to my chin. The oil smelled earthy. Next, he lit a slender stick on fire. He pushed the smoke at me with a feather and started saying a blessing.

Pent-up anger raged within me, charging up my spine, and coming out in a scream that sounded inhuman.

Beside me, Kade held tight to my hand.

I tried to pull away, but he held me firm. "Come back to me, Riley. Please...I need you. Your family needs you. We all love you so much."

Dot placed her hands over me as well, and I felt heat radiating from them.

Angus started shaking a rattle over me. He made me furious. I wanted to yank the damn thing out of his hand. My nails dug in my palms.

"There is a very strong entity attached to her," Dot said.

I heard Laria's voice calling to me...and even though my eyes were closed, I saw her. Her face so near mine, her features just out of focus. Her lips curved in a cruel smile, and her brown eyes turned a glowing red.

Her face shifted and I saw gaping black holes where her eyes should be.

The shaman's voice grew louder, and my body shook so badly, I was ready to vibrate right off the end of the bed.

"Get those fucking rocks off of me," I said in a voice I didn't recognize.

My eyes flew open and Miss Akin made the sign of the cross.

I felt my body leave the bed.

"Oh my God." This time it was Shane.

"I need everyone to help," Angus said to them, and soon I had hands holding me down, pulling me back toward the bed.

"Leave her alone!" Kade yelled, sounding equally furious and desperate.

"I call upon the spirit who is possessing this woman to step forward," Dot said with authority. "Answer me and tell me your name."

A wave of nausea washed over me, hitting me with a force that stunned me. I felt Laria inside me, like small tendrils of smoke working its way up my body, pushing from my feet upward, and I couldn't stop trembling. "Laria," I said, and once again it wasn't in my voice.

"You are not allowed to torment this young woman any longer." Angus shook the rattle over my body.

Sweat poured off me, rolling off my forehead and onto the bed.

"Leave her," Dot said, hand pressed against my forehead. "Leave her now."

A horrible laugh came out of me, followed by words in an unknown language.

"There is not just one within her." Dot's voice sounded ominous. "There are many...evil entities who practiced dark arts when they were in human form." She took a deep breath in, closed her eyes for a moment. "His name is Randall. He is nasty. So evil."

"What do they want?" Kade asked.

"Revenge," Dot said abruptly. Her brows furrowed and she looked off toward the wall. "Riley knew these individuals in another life."

"She's talked about a past life with Ian, who was an ancestor of mine," Kade said. "I was in that life with her."

"Ah, I see," Dot said quietly.

Everyone went silent, and I knew they were trying to process what was being said. I was so relieved Dot was validating the truth not just for me, but for my family and Kade.

Dot's breathing became more even and deeper. "Sometimes life does not make sense," she said, "but you were all drawn back to this place for a reason."

A chill rushed through me at her words. I lifted further off the bed, my body board straight, but they held me down.

"Our souls go around together, time and time again, in different capacities—sometimes within the same family, sometimes as friends or acquaintances." Dot rested her hand on my forehead. "Riley resided in Braemar and was in contact with these individuals. Spirit tells me you were all there. All of this did not happen by chance. This was predestined. Unfinished business, so to speak."

Screams sounded throughout the house, louder by the second, and I wondered why no one else was saying anything. Couldn't they hear them?

"There was a double murder that took place many, many years ago at the castle where I live," Kade said, and I was surprised he was so forthcoming. "The man who was murdered was me."

Shane whistled under his breath.

Dot smiled. "You will all remember those lives, young man, and then release that which no longer serves you."

I saw a vision of the table that night when Ian was poisoned, the people there. Although the faces weren't the ones I knew in this lifetime, I suddenly saw each person as who they are now—today's equivalent. Shane had been Duncan, Cait had been one of Ian's sisters, Maddy had been the other. Kade's father was a head servant, the one who had helped haul Laria out to the tree and string her up. The servants in the house were Megan, Cass, even Miss Akin. We were all there...in some capacity.

The only one not accounted for was Maggie, Ian's mother, until there was a flash of light and then I saw Karen's face. I smiled inwardly. Ian and his mom had another chance to live a life as mother and son.

A bright light flashed, and a sense of peace came over me, rolling through me in waves.

I could hear what was happening in the room, but I saw an ethereal woman staring down at me. It was hard to make out her features because of the blinding light that haloed her. I knew that silhouette. I would know it anywhere.

"Mom," I said the word on a sob.

I heard Shane's quick intake of breath.

My mom's hands were on my forehead, her face above me, and she whispered, "You're all right, Riley. You'll be fine, sweetheart. You are protected. The angels are with you. I am with you, and you will never have to fear those dark spirits again."

The warmth was incredible. She felt like a warm blanket, sliding around me, comforting me, pushing out the negative. Pushing out Laria, Randall, and the others.

A kaleidoscope of colors flashed before my eyes. Beautiful shades of purples, blues, pinks, greens. Over and over again, comforting me.

"We cut all cords that tie Riley to these spirits." The shaman's hands were moving fast now.

Peace. I felt so much peace, and when I opened my eyes, Angus was looking down at me, a wide smile on his face. "How do you feel?"

I blinked a few times, looked down at my body that was no longer levitating off the bed. All the anger and depression were gone. "Fine."

Miss A had an I-can't-believe-what-I-just-experienced expression on her face. Shane was grinning, and still talking to Dad.

Kade looked elated, and as relieved as Miss A and Shane. His hands cupped my face and he kissed me softly. "I love you."

"I love you, too." I threw my arms around him and cried. He held me so tight, I had a tough time taking a breath.

"You're okay." He said the words like he couldn't quite believe it.

Tears in my eyes, I looked over his shoulder and saw Peter and Anne Marie. I couldn't help but smile.

I owed Peter a huge apology. I'd treated him like crap, and he'd turned around and saved me from jumping off the roof.

Miss A straightened and looked in the direction I was staring. "Who is it?"

I glanced at her and smiled. "Anne Marie and Peter."

Miss A's hands flew to her face. "I knew it."

"Peter. You mean the boy from the roof?" Shane asked.

"Yes."

"Thank you, Peter," Shane said, looking in the direction of Peter and Anne Marie.

Peter smiled, and Anne Marie ruffled his hair.

Finally, Peter was able to come to me, to my house, because he would not be kept away by fear of Laria, Randall, or the others.

Angus and Dot said a closing prayer and when they finished, they blessed and cleansed the inn, burning white sage—smudging as they called it—which helped to keep the energy clean and clear.

Before she left, Dot gave me a blessed charm. "I want you to keep it...to help with protection. Those of us who work with spirits must be extremely careful what we open ourselves up to."

She wasn't kidding.

"Thank you."

Dot squeezed my shoulder. "Now you have one final thing to do."

"What's that?" I asked.

She smiled softly. "Give her peace."

Chapter Twenty-Three

I was surrounded by my brother and our friends. Kade, Cait, Megan, Milo, Richie, and Cass had come with me and Shane to the hillside. Finally, the weather had cleared. In fact, the sun was shining, but there was a definite chill to the air. Fall was coming fast.

"We stay together," Kade said, sliding his cell phone into his jeans pocket. "No exceptions, regardless."

Everyone had a backpack, and as we started out over the rough terrain, I felt the presence of the others with us. Since the cleansing, I felt more like my old self, and I knew I was protected. My mom was with me, and Anne Marie was too. I saw her more frequently, and Miss A seemed to especially like the idea that her friend was around. Peter had stayed on the periphery. I didn't blame him. Until Laria was gone, he would probably be scarce.

God willing, today was the day Laria would be stopped forever.

Shane slid his knife into the side pocket of the backpack. "I think we have everything that we need."

We walked to the cemetery without saying a word to each other.

This was just so much to take in.

I'd slept peacefully for the first time since Laria had first appeared, and I was so relieved. Relieved to know that there was resolution in sight and that life would return to some semblance of normal.

Kade reached for my hand, his fingers threading through mine. "You ready?" He had proven to me just how much he cared during the cleansing, and I knew if we could get through this, then we could get through anything.

I made a final mental note of the things we had brought along for the binding ceremony. Angus and Dot had given me everything I needed. I only hoped that I didn't mess it up. Dot repeated several times to me that driving a nail into the grave was the physical part of the intention. It was the intention itself that needed to be clear and concise, and all of us needed to be in the same mindset.

Every single one of us wanted this over with, and I was proud of my friends for taking a stand with me.

We were heading into the woods when Maddy raced toward us.

She was dressed to hike, and even had a backpack on.

"No way, squirt, you're not going," Kade said, and Cait nodded in agreement.

"I want to," Maddy said adamantly. "Plus, I can help you."

I felt Hanway's presence. I always thought he couldn't leave the castle, but I wondered if he would be able to leave if he thought that Maddy truly needed him.

I had so many misgivings about her going. What if something went wrong? Then again, since she was also psychic, she would be able to see, feel, and hear everything as well, which could prove helpful.

"I'll tell Aunt Karen and Uncle Dustin what you're doing if you don't take me," she said, sounding downright bratty.

"Fair enough, she comes with," Shane said.

Cait shook her head, but didn't argue.

Cass looked ready for a weekend of skiing in Aspen with her fur-lined boots and stylish jacket, but far be it from me to say anything. I was just glad to have her. She had mentioned to me that she was over Johan after hearing he'd been making out with another chick in the laundry room at her party.

Maybe she was finally getting over him. I hoped she realized she deserved better.

I still think there was something between her and Tom, and I wondered if one day anything would transpire between the two.

We walked in silence for a good fifteen minutes.

Laria knew we were coming. I felt it in my bones. Felt her fury. I slid my hand in my pocket and touched the blessed charm for reassurance.

The forest had a dark dreariness to it that was hard to shake off. I could feel Laria's resentment, her hatred toward me with every step.

"It's over here." There was a small pathway that led straight into the overgrown brush.

I recognized the pathway from my dreams.

Shane pushed through. "The brush is pretty dense."

Kade removed his backpack, pulled out a knife. He went to town on the brush, making easy work of it and forging a path with the help of Shane, Milo, and Richie, who all pitched in to help.

I was impressed by the teamwork.

Following the crude pathway, we made our way deeper in.

Maddy reached for my hand, making me wonder if she was feeling the uneasiness, too. I got a sense she regretted that she had come.

From the corner of my eye, I saw a black figure rush from one tree to the next.

I couldn't afford for Laria to get the upper hand again. It would destroy me mentally. I stopped and reached for Kade, who followed my gaze. "They're here."

Chanting began and I turned to Maddy to see if she heard it too.

Her hand tightened around mine.

Cait went completely still. In fact, all of us went completely quiet.

Cass took a step closer to Megan, and wrapped a hand around her elbow. "Tell me that's not what I think it is."

"Don't freak out," Shane said adamantly. "Angus said they will thrive off our fear."

Cass straightened her spine and lifted her chin a few inches, while reaching into the inside jacket pocket with her free hand.

She pulled out pepper spray.

Cait opened her mouth to say something but I shook my head. If pepper spray gave her peace of mind, then let her use it.

"Remember that stone you were telling me about?" Kade said. "Is that it?"

We all turned toward where Kade was looking. There was the same basketball-sized stone I'd seen in the dream.

It was a grave. Laria's grave. I nodded. I was surprised by the strange emotions that rushed through me, most of all relief.

Maddy looked up at me, eyes wide. "Do you see them?"

"No, but I feel them. Do you see them?"

She nodded.

"Where are they, Maddy?" Cait asked.

Maddy motioned over toward our left. "Over there. This is a graveyard."

I remembered what the blonde-haired woman who had been sacrificed had said to me...*You find her and you find them all.*

"Hanway said that the village wanted an end to the sacrifices, so they killed all of the witches in the coven." Maddy shifted on her feet. "They're all buried here. The witches...and their victims."

Megan and Cass looked ready to run back down the hillside.

"Let's do this," Kade said, sliding his backpack off.

Everyone followed his lead.

"We're protected," I said to my friends, knowing that even though we were surrounded by Laria, Randall, and the other witches, we also had spirits that were guiding us.

Our team was stronger than theirs.

I suddenly felt that same sense of peace that had come over me the other night when my mom had shown up. I felt her strength, and I felt Anne Marie, too, and every spirit who had been killed by this coven.

I dropped my backpack and started rummaging through it. Kade pulled out the hammer, the bag of nails, and I removed the blessed charm.

"Hold hands," I heard my mom say.

"We need to hold hands," I told my friends.

We all held hands. Before we'd set out, we'd talked about intention. We spoke the words, said the blessing, and I drove the nail into the ground. One by one, with the spirit of my mother guiding us, we did all the things we were supposed to do.

There was no scream, no movement at all that gave us a sign that we had succeeded.

"Are we done?" Megan asked, sounding surprised it had been so easy.

I nodded, and everyone grabbed their backpacks and with a final glance at the grave, headed back the way we had come.

Kade took my hand, and we started walking, but I stopped short.

"What's wrong?" he asked.

"Dot told me to give her peace. I need to send them to the other side," I said, knowing with a certainty that's what I had to do.

Everyone ahead of us had turned to look back.

"We'll be right behind you," I said, hoping to reassure them that everything was okay.

"No way," Shane said. "We came up together, we go down together."

My friends all agreed.

I felt guided by a force so much larger than myself. The words I said were simple. I asked for Laria, Randall, and the rest of those who were not at peace, to be escorted into the light. I asked my friends to close their eyes and envision the white light and to say a prayer for their passing.

It was so strange, because all the fear and anger I felt toward Laria evaporated in that moment. I knew my life would never be the same because of what we'd gone through. I would never take the spirit world for granted because of her.

She had haunted me for months now, and I was ready to put it behind me forever. I had a new appreciation for the world of the dead. I knew that life went on after we die...and those who choose to stay and not move on have more power over the living than I could have ever imagined.

Just as there were bad people, there were bad spirits.

A shiver rushed along my spine and I knew Laria stood behind me. I felt the coldness first, and half expected her to grab me by the back of the neck and start choking me. Instead, she came up beside me, and I glanced over at her. She looked different to me. Softer, and for the first time I didn't fear her.

"*Go to the light, Laria,*" I said.

The wind whipped her hair, and she lifted her chin and looked out over the valley, toward the castle. I remembered Ian's fear at leaving Braemar after being earthbound for two centuries. I saw that same fear in Laria's eyes.

"*I'm afraid,*" she said. "*This is all I've ever known.*"

"*Why would you want to stay?*"

"*I fear what's waiting for me.*"

I didn't know what waited for her, but I felt in my heart it was better than being stuck here, wreaking havoc on the living. "*You deserve to have peace. It has been a long time coming.*"

She was as surprised by my words as I was.

"*I loved him,*" she said. I didn't have to ask who we were talking about. I knew it was Ian. "*He was incredibly charming.*"

I smiled. I remembered that charm firsthand.

"*I never meant to kill him. The others told me that the poison would only make him sick, like it had made you sick. I wanted to take care of him. To ease him back to health and then he would want me because I had cared for him.*"

That surprised me. All this time she had been such a malevolent presence, and I had assumed she'd intentionally killed Ian. "*What about Randall?*"

"*He told me he had power, and then he showed me. I was intrigued by him, but I didn't love him.*"

Laria glanced over at Kade who, like the rest of my friends, had his eyes closed. "*He loves you.*"

I nodded. "*I know. And I love him, too.*"

For the first time she genuinely smiled. "*It's time for me to go,*" she said, and I felt the pull of the other side, the pulsing bright light that seemed to call to her.

She walked toward it, and then slowly Randall and the others followed behind her. The blonde woman who had been the coven's victim walked past. *"Thank you,"* she said, a beautiful smile on her face.

My breath left me in a rush.

I heard a gasp. Maddy's eyes were wide open and she blinked back tears.

Anne Marie turned to me. *"You did it, kid."*

"I couldn't have done it without you." I could only hope I didn't have anything to do with her death.

"I think I'll follow...just to be sure they stay where they're going."

"Like an escort?"

"More like a guard," she said, her laughter like music to my ears. *"I'm ready to go home, to see my spirit family. They've been calling me."*

"Anne Marie, did you die because of—"

She rested her hand on my shoulder. *"The answer is no. Do you hear me?"*

I nodded.

"I had been sick for a while. I just didn't want to tell anyone."

I think she was just being nice. True, she might have been sick, but I knew that spirits had a tendency to drain the living, and if you were frail at all, you were seriously in danger of becoming depleted energy-wise.

She glanced toward the light that grew brighter. *"I must go now."*

"Visit me," I said. *"And Miss Akin. She'll want to see you again."*

"I'll see you both...in your dreams," she said with a wink, and then she walked into the light, and it closed around her.

"You did it, sweetheart."

Mom squeezed my shoulder. I smiled, knowing she would be with me. Knowing I would feel this, the intense love that surrounded me and filled every single sense. I wished I could feel this way forever.

I had done it...but not without her help. She had saved me more than once, and I was so incredibly grateful.

"*Never leave me, Mom.*"

"*Not a chance, sweetheart.*"

I closed my eyes, took a deep breath and said a thank you before I turned back to my friends. Kade smiled wide and my heart squeezed with love for him. I was holding onto that man with both hands.

Chapter Twenty-Four

woke up to the sun shining through the gap in the curtains, nearly blinding me. Before I could blink, I knew I wasn't alone.

I glanced at Peter, who was sitting in the chair, where he had no doubt been waiting for me to wake up for hours. Every single morning he was there, anxious to spend time with me.

"I thought I told you I wanted to sleep in today."

Peter glanced at the clock and shrugged. "It's eleven."

I sat up straight. "Eleven! How could you let me sleep so long?"

His shoulders sagged and I laughed. "It's not your fault, but I do need to get cleaned up."

I jumped up, rushed to the bathroom, and turned on the shower. We had a strict policy that the bathroom was off-limits, a rule he had no problem with.

Peter had become a fixture in my life, though we had to set up some boundaries, especially at school. He couldn't interfere or help me with schoolwork, unless of course I asked for it. Now that Laria and the others were gone, he roamed Braemar freely.

It had been three months since my friends and I had helped Laria and the coven pass over, and life had fallen into a new normal. An incredible normal that had me looking forward to the future. I hadn't cut at all in the months since Laria left, and though there were times I thought about it, if the urge arose, I talked to Kade, Shane, or one of my friends, and I always felt better.

I took a quick shower, got dressed, put on makeup, and was drying my hair when Shane popped his head in. "Happy birthday, Ri."

"Thanks, Shane."

"Dad wants to talk to you when you get a sec."

My eyes widened.

He laughed. "Don't worry, you're not in trouble. He probably just wants to know where you want to go for your birthday dinner."

"I'll be down in ten."

"Sounds good."

The second he closed the door, I turned to Peter who was sprawled in the chair. "Are you sure you don't want to go into the light today?" I asked. "With it being my birthday and all?"

He shook his head. "Nah, not today."

There wouldn't be a day when I didn't ask him. He wasn't ready to leave, and truth be told, I don't think I was ready to let him go either. He was actually helpful to me, especially when it came to my lessons with Dot, who had become my mentor. We met once a week, and I had learned so much from her already. I could hardly wait to see what the future would bring.

"You'd better get downstairs," Peter said when I finished curling my hair.

He was right. I glanced at the clock. I'd been longer than ten minutes.

He walked with me, and when we got to the kitchen no one was there. In fact, Miss A hadn't cooked anything.

I frowned.

Peter shrugged.

We walked into the dining room.

"Surprise!" My family—including Miss A and Cheryl—were here, along with all my friends.

"Happy birthday," they said in unison.

"Awww, thanks," I said, thrilled to see them all standing around the dining room table, where a large sheet cake with red roses read *Happy 17th Birthday, Riley.*

"Kade bought it," Cait said, a wide smile on her face as she glanced at her brother, who grinned and gave me a kiss.

"I couldn't resist," he said. "I saw it and I thought of you and a poem by Robert Burns called *A Red, Red Rose.*"

My throat tightened. Ian had left that poem for me in a book. "My love is like a red, red rose," I quoted the opening line.

"Well done, Ri," Milo said with a wink. "I think the Scottish life is rubbing off on you a bit."

"Just a wee bit," I said in a Scottish accent, and everyone laughed.

Dad walked over to me, reached inside his pocket, and produced a key. "Happy birthday, Riley."

"You didn't," I said, shocked that my dad had bought me a car, especially when I had a ways to go on getting my license. I was taking lessons, though, and soon I would be free to drive the windy roads of Braemar.

"Well," Dad said. "I wanted you to wear the brakes out on your own car, and not mine."

Kade grinned and I elbowed him. "What's so funny?" I couldn't hide my smile. I did have a tendency to brake hard.

I gave Dad a hug, and Cheryl as well. Cheryl had made a positive difference in all our lives. Mom had told me that she had put Cheryl in Dad's path because he needed her. Maybe we *all* needed her. Kind of like Miss A.

She was stuck with us for life now.

Dad pressed the key into my hand. "Go...look."

Everyone followed me to the door.

A cute, navy car sat in the driveway.

It had some years on it, but I didn't care. It was mine and I was thrilled.

"An elderly woman out of Ballater owned it for six years," Dad said, chest puffing out with pride. "It only has eight thousand kilometers on it. Can you believe it?"

Shane opened the driver's side door and looked in. "Sweet!"

I gave my dad a hug.

"Happy birthday, sweetheart," he said, kissing me on the forehead.

"Thanks, Dad. I love it."

Our relationship had changed in a huge way. He looked at me differently. I think everyone did, and I looked at them differently, too. I was at home here. It made sense; I had lived here once before. Braemar was a part of me. I had met the love of my life and had lifelong friends, and I wasn't going anywhere.

"Um, everyone better get out of the way," I said.

"I hate to burst your bubble, but I'm going to have to go with you for a test drive." Dad rolled back on his heels. "Or maybe Kade can take you."

He didn't have to say it twice. I raced to the passenger's side, and slid in, while Kade took a seat behind the wheel.

Kade started the car and everyone cheered.

He put the car in drive and looked at me. "So...where do you want to go?"

I shrugged. "I don't know…how about we go to the river?"

I had lost my virginity at the river, and to me it would always hold that significance and the incredible memory of making love to the man I loved and adored.

Kade's lips curved into a slow, wolfish smile. I felt my entire body go hot at that stare. "It might be kind of cold."

I shrugged. "I'm sure you can keep me warm."

His blue eyes smoldered. "Now that's an invitation I can't resist."

Books by

J. A. Templeton

The Deepest Cut (a MacKinnon Curse novel, book one)
The Haunted (a MacKinnon Curse novel, book two)
The MacKinnon Curse novella (The Beginning)

———

If you enjoyed this story, you might also enjoy
the following YA novels:
Brightest Kind of Darkness by P.T. Michelle
In Dreams by J. Sterling

About the Author

J.A. Templeton writes young adult novels featuring characters that don't necessarily fit into any box. Aside from writing and reading, she enjoys research, traveling, riding motorcycles, and spending time with family and friends. Married to her high school sweetheart, she has two grown children and lives in Washington. Visit her website www.jatempleton.com for the most updated information on new releases. She loves hearing from readers!

8674923R00126

Made in the USA
San Bernardino, CA
17 February 2014